I0769203

FATAL
BETRAYAL

SHANNON HOLLINGER

This book is dedicated to all the pygmy goats.
I'm waiting for you with open arms.

CHAPTER 1

I jolt awake, heart pounding, gasping for air, but for once, it's not the fingers of a nightmare clawing at my nerves. The sensation that usually lingers after I've revisited that dank basement where I was chained by a serial killer isn't there. Which means that something else woke me.

My skin prickles as I search the darkened room with wide eyes, peering into the shadows. Nothing's there. My breathing slows. The rush of my pulse eases in my ears. And that's when I hear the faint tinkle of breaking glass.

Immediately, my gaze darts to the bedroom door, barely visible through the murky haze of night. But I can see it well enough to tell that it's open. Closing it hadn't seemed necessary, since there's no one here other than me. Correction—there *was* no one here but me. Now? I realize the advantages of a shut door.

My muscles twist into knots as I inch my way to the edge of the bed. Sweat runs in ticklish drops across my overheated flesh. Knocking against something, I reach out to catch it but miss, cursing silently as my Kindle hits the carpet with a muffled thud. I follow it a moment later as I slide from beneath the covers, lowering myself to the floor.

Pulling on my clothes from the day before, I know I

need a plan. I'm supposed to be laying low, staying out of trouble right now. Even if I weren't, the thought of going out there and confronting whoever is breaking into my home right now makes me feel ill. I'm not sure that I can do it.

But what other options do I have? My eyes drift to the window, the dresser beneath it covered with a tower of clothing and assorted junk. It's the only way out of this room, this house, that doesn't involve encountering whoever is out there. I don't even know if it opens, much less how I'd attempt to get out of it quietly if it did. The odds aren't good.

And the interior doors in this house are hollow. You could break through them with a violent sneeze. Even if I crept across the room and closed it, locking the door won't keep whoever this is out—not if they want in.

The way I see it, I only have one option. Is it smart? Probably not.

Do I want to do it? Not at all.

But I don't think I have a choice.

I can stay here, waiting to be discovered. Or I can go on the offensive. Use the one thing I have going for me right now—the element of surprise—to my advantage.

The static in my head is deafening as I try to talk some sense into myself, and yet still I hear the soft creak as the door to my grandfather's room across the hall opens. But they won't find anything in there. Since Butch died a couple of weeks ago, I've cleaned it out, donated everything to a charity shop. Which means they won't be in there long. I need to move while I have the chance.

My legs wobble beneath me as I stand, my entire body trembling as fear and adrenaline collide. I keep my eyes on the dark gap of the open door as I shove my feet into a pair of tennis shoes and slink to my closet. Hold my breath as I ease it open, muscles twitching as I rise to my toes, wrapping my hands around the metal box on the shelf.

Raising the lid, the gun within, Butch's old snubnosed .357 revolver, catches what little moonlight that's filtered in between the gap in the curtains. It seems to glow as I lift it from its foam bed, the thumb of my right hand pulling back the hammer as my left hand abandons the now empty box on my bed and grabs my cell from the nightstand.

I put my phone on Do Not Disturb mode so it won't make noise or vibrate, then as much as I don't want to, I text 911 that there's a home invasion in progress at my address. It's a necessary evil.

My history with the local sheriff is long and thorny. As much as I hate giving him a reason to think he's coming to my rescue, I dread giving him an excuse to legitimately harass me even more. If I fire this weapon, I better be able to prove that I at least attempted to let him handle the problem first.

Slipping the device into my back pocket, I draw a deep breath in, hold it for five seconds before slowly releasing it to steady my nerves. Then I tiptoe out into the hall.

I try to build my confidence by assuring myself that whoever broke into my house made a huge mistake.

I'm not going to run. Or hide. This isn't the first monster I've encountered.

There's a reason my demons haunt me. It's because I killed them.

I'm not saying that whoever this is has to die. Just that if I have to choose between one of us, it won't be me.

But my tough thoughts aren't working. My legs tremble beneath me. Dizziness has me firmly in its grasp. As an FBI agent, I know I should be braver than this.

I was, once. But that was before. Now? I'm terrified. And I need to pee.

Suspense makes my anxiety skyrocket as I stand there, watching the door to Butch's room, wondering what's taking them so long. There's nothing in there, just a box of mementos shoved into the corner. So what are they doing? Afraid I'll pass out before they emerge, I force myself to find out.

Keeping my elbows bent, the barrel of the gun aimed toward the ceiling, I put one foot carefully in front of the other, stalking forward. Pause in the doorway, trying to make sense of what I'm seeing. A figure dressed in black kneels on the carpet, facing the corner. Are they really riffling through the box of my grandfather's keepsakes?

Enraged at the mere idea of them touching Butch's things, I level the gun and summon my voice. "FBI. Raise your hands in the air and turn around. Slowly."

Their back goes rigid as my words shatter the silence. Their head turns until they're looking at me over their shoulder. Though I strain to make out their face, I can't, it's too dark. All I can see is the glitter of a pair of eyes peering at me from under the shelter of a hoodie—but they seem entirely too calm for someone who broke into a house and now has a firearm aimed at them.

"I said—"

I realize my mistake a moment too late. I'm not even retired yet, and I've forgotten the basics. I've failed to clear the room.

An image of the headline flashes through my mind—FBI AGENT KILLED IN HER OWN HOME—as I spin toward the en suite bathroom just as a second figure lunges from inside, their hands grabbing for my weapon.

I vaguely register their partner in crime leaping to

their feet to join the fray as we wrestle over it. Driving my elbow into their ribs once, twice, three times as I try to loosen their grip, I know my luck is running out.

Wrapping my calf around one of theirs, I transfer all my weight to it as I use my elbow a fourth time, this time rotating with the action. The force of it drives them back, my knee torquing painfully as they trip over my leg just as a second pair of hands shoves against me, slamming me into the wall. I fall to my knees, avoiding the heavy-duty flashlight that crashes into the spot where my head just was by such a narrow margin that the breeze of the strike ruffles my hair.

My skull throbs, dark bubbles popping along the edges of my vision. Nausea thins my spit. All I can see is the glint of the window across from me. I aim for it and pull the trigger. It shatters instantly.

The motion around me goes deathly still as both assailants freeze. Even though the revolver is double-action, and it isn't necessary to shoot, I pull the hammer back again to accentuate my point. Raise my voice to hear myself over the ringing in my ears as I swing the firearm in their direction and growl, "Get out. Now."

I listen as two pairs of shoes race from the room. Getting to my feet, I stagger after them, following at a distance, making sure they both leave. Though it seems pointless, I close and lock the front door after them, peering through the broken pane. I can't see their vehicle, but the night turns red with their taillights. And then they're gone.

Two weeks ago, I'd be stuck in the throes of a panic attack after what just happened. That was then. Now? I'm shocked to realize that what I feel is absolutely furious.

CHAPTER 2

I crack my knuckles. My teeth grind together so hard it feels like I'm trying to make diamonds. And when I catch the eyeroll aimed in my direction, it takes everything I have to keep my feet on the ground instead of launching myself through the air in attack mode. He just got here and already the man in front of me is making my mood worse.

Sheriff Lyle Kingston scowls at me as he climbs out of his cruiser, his glare making it clear exactly how much he resents being pulled from his bed in the middle of the night to respond to my 911 call. I'm sure the fact that it was made by me, the girl from the swamp who had the audacity to not just date, but escape, his son Matt decades ago hasn't helped.

Well, too bad. It's not like I want him here. In fact, as soon as my adrenaline had eased enough for me to calm down and think clearly again, I'd started hoping that anyone but him would be dispatched.

But once I realized how much time had passed since I'd placed the request for help without an officer showing, I knew that my luck had run out for the night. I adjust the ice pack I'm holding against the tender side of my face so he can see me return his contempt.

"Cassidy Knox," he drawls, crossing his arms as he leans against the side of his vehicle. Just the sound of his voice saying my name makes my irritation grow. "I didn't expect to see you again so soon."

"It wasn't by choice, I assure you."

"Then why make the call?"

"I suppose I thought you might want to know about criminal activity going on in your town."

"That the way they got in?" he asks, gesturing toward the broken pane of glass in the door behind me.

"Yes."

"What'd they take?"

"I don't think they got anything."

He snorts.

"What?"

"Nothing." Then, smirking, "Just surprised an FBI agent like yourself would make such a big deal out of what was probably just a couple of kids pulling a prank."

"A prank? Back when I was a kid in this town, a prank was Vaseline on a door handle or painting someone's cow, not breaking into someone's house at three in the morning while they're sleeping. These weren't kids."

"Did you see their faces?"

"No."

"Then how can you be sure?"

"Because kids wouldn't attack an armed homeowner if they got caught 'pulling a prank.'"

"Times change. Can't be sure what kids these days would or wouldn't do. They probably panicked when you showed up waving a gun in their faces."

"I wasn't—" I close my mouth. Take a deep breath, trying to calm down. "Next time, what would you suggest I do, Lyle?" His eyes narrow as I use his first name. "It took you over forty minutes to respond. Let's just say for a minute that these weren't kids. What do you think would have happened if I hadn't been armed?"

"You probably would have done the smart thing and locked yourself in a room."

"The interior doors are hollow. They won't stop anyone who wants past them."

His gaze once again falls to the glass panel in the door that the would-be thieves broke to get inside. "You ask me, what you need is a man around the house," he says.

But I didn't ask him. And in case he hasn't noticed, it's not the 1950s anymore. I bite my tongue and give him a disgusted look, but he's either not smart enough or too dense to read it.

The sheriff sneers as he adds, "Guess things didn't work out between you and that swamp scum chump you were shacking up with."

"He's in the hospital," I say. "Recovering from the bullet he took saving my life."

Or has the sheriff forgotten already? It's been less than a week since he came out here—uninvited that time—to the scene of a crime that the state police responded to. Or maybe that visit had nothing to do with his job, since all he accomplished while he was here was to make it clear that I wasn't welcome in his town.

But I grew up here in Gator Glade. I'm the same "swamp scum," as he's so eloquently been putting it my entire life, as Jake. My grandfather left me the animal sanctuary he ran. And I have no plans to leave. So whatever issues Sheriff Kingston has with me, he's going to have to get over them, because I'm not going anywhere.

"I'm just saying. You're tempting fate. A woman shouldn't be out here alone on her own like this."

He hawks a loogie and I make a mental note to bleach the yard once the sun comes up, wishing I'd never made the call. Had I known how the night would turn out, I doubt I would have made the same decision.

But I was scared. And I suppose thinking that help was on the way made my fear less crippling.

What he *should* be doing is taking photographs, checking for evidence, taking casts of shoe and tire impressions, documenting the scene in hopes of making an arrest and prosecuting a crime, not spitting all over it and blaming me for what's happened because I'm a woman living alone. It's not like I have a big neon sign flashing out by the road announcing it.

Sighing, I decide to make one last attempt at helping him do his job. "Would you like me to send you a copy of the surveillance footage?" I ask.

"Does it show their plate number?"

"No."

"The make and model of their vehicle?"

"Nope."

"A clear shot of their faces?"

"Uh-uh."

"Then I don't see what good it will do."

My stomach complains as I swallow down a piping hot knot of anger. True, the video of the perps breaking in isn't going to hand him the identities of the people involved on a silver platter, but even when the answers aren't given to you, crimes still get solved. It's called police work. But I guess if I expect any of that to get done around here, I'll be doing it myself.

"Maybe you can have some of your FBI friends give you a hand, help you solve the Case of the Kiddie Caper."

I grit my teeth behind the fake smile I force, not wanting to let him see how much he's gotten under my skin as he lowers himself back inside his cruiser with a grunt.

"In the meantime, take my advice. At the very least,

throw a pair of Butch's old boots on the front porch so it looks like there's a man around. I don't want to have to come back out here any time soon."

He closes the door and starts the engine. Gives me a mock salute through the window before putting the car in gear and pulling a wide circle back to the driveway. As soon as he's gone, I flick a double salute back at him and let loose with a string of words that would make a sailor's parrot blush.

Whoever broke in, they weren't kids. Whatever they were after, they didn't get it. Which means I need to figure out who they are and what they want, because the sick feeling in my gut is telling me that they'll be back.

CHAPTER 3

It's a horrible thing, to be so utterly alone. And I don't just mean how isolated I am out here in the middle of the swamp. I mean alone, alone.

With Jake laid up in the hospital, and local law enforcement clearly not interested in helping, there's no one I can count on besides myself. I know for a fact that fear can become crippling if you let it.

And though I'm determined not to let it, right now I'd almost choose another conversation with Sheriff Kingston just to distract myself from feeling so desperate. Almost.

Then I see it. A sudden burst of hope surges through me, leaving me vibrating. Leaning back in my seat, I stretch my spine and mutter, "Gotcha."

Not really. Not yet, anyway. But I've got something, which is a start.

Junior year of college, my roommate talked me into taking a kinesiology class with her second term. She argued all the real-life applications while she was trying to convince me to join her, and as a criminal justice major, I couldn't deny that there was a chance I could learn something that might come in handy one day.

I just didn't understand how she, as an economics student, would benefit—at least, not until the first day when she sat next to me drooling over the TA who taught it the entire time. By then, there was no point in trying to transfer to a different course. All the ones I'd been interested in were already full. So I'd decided to make the most of it.

Now, I'm glad that I did. I get up and pour myself another cup of coffee, stifling a yawn as I glance into the living room at Stephano, the pygmy goat, curled into a ball in the corner of the couch, sound asleep. I know I'm going to regret letting him come inside, but when he came trotting over from the barn as Sheriff Kingston drove off, I couldn't resist.

It's a miracle that he hadn't woken while the intruders were here. He could have been hurt—or worse. We both could have been. I'd been so relieved that we'd all escaped serious injury that I couldn't bring myself to carry the little escape artist back to his stall. And maybe a small part of me craved the companionship as well.

Because I can't stand feeling vulnerable, but until I figure out who broke into my house, and why, that's exactly what I am. It's clear that the sheriff isn't taking the threat seriously. Which means it's up to me to find the answers.

My eyes drift from Stephano down to the faded stain on the front of the couch—the one made by Jake's blood after he was shot. Every time I see it, it's a reminder of the danger I've put those around me in because of my past mistakes.

And when my gaze hits the missing rectangle of carpet on the floor below it, removed because it was soaked in the shooter's blood, I feel the pressure to stay sharp and get answers before it's too late. I can't let what happened last time repeat itself.

Returning to my seat at the kitchen table, I pull my laptop closer, adjust the screen, then press play, watching the duo who broke into my house on the surveillance footage for the dozenth time.

They approach from the west, by the driveway, entering the frame with the casual abandon of someone who doesn't know they're being recorded. The one in the lead is taller than the other, with a broader build and confident swagger. His head is turned over his shoulder, toward his companion. He runs a gloved hand through his hair as he approaches the door, before pulling his hoodie up.

I freeze the frame, icy fingers tickling up my spine as I take in the plain white mask he wears once again, despite the number of times I've already seen it. It's not just that the thing is creepy, though it definitely is. It's that somehow, as inexplicable as it seems, I know that he's smiling behind it.

What they're about to do? Breaking into someone's home? He enjoys it.

His body language gives me a good sense of who I'm looking at—a man who's no stranger to crime. His kinesiology, or movement, suggests that he's under forty and in good physical condition. His shoes, distinctive enough in the grainy black-and-white video to suggest they'd be downright flashy in full color, along with his cocky mannerisms, lead me to believe his age to be under thirty.

It's a full six seconds later that his accomplice appears. At first glance, I thought this signified reluctance, but when they reach the doorstep, they elbow the man out of their way, taking charge and using the heavy-duty flashlight they carry, the same one they swung at my head, to break the window.

This one, I decide, is older. It's not just how they take charge, or how the other one seems to cede to their authority. It's not even how the younger one had wrestled me for my gun almost like it was a game, while this one had dealt what would have been a crushing, incapacitating—if not fatal—blow, had it actually hit me.

I chug half of my fresh mug of coffee even though it's too hot, the scalding heat opening my eyes just as wide as the burst of caffeine, and watch the clip again. Make sure that I'm not just imagining it. Because this second person? They have a limp.

It's minor, but it's distinctive. Though they have the same eerie blank mask disguising their face as their companion does, their gait is a feature I feel confident I'd recognize if I saw it again.

While the right leg strides cleanly, the left leg has a slight hitch, as if its owner has to swing it forward. That, coupled with a slight stoop of the shoulders, makes me think this one is over fifty. I can't rule out that what I've noticed is the result of an injury, but I also can't detect anything else identifiable about either of them. It's all I've got, so for now, I'm sticking with it.

My vision blurs as I stare at the screen, willing it to tell me more. When it doesn't, I take pity on my exhausted eyes and look away. Realize with relief that it's finally late enough to call my supervisor, Director in Charge Marla Jacobson, and let her know what's happened.

Pushing back from the table, I wonder what I'll do when I don't have her to turn to anymore as I dial. The time's coming. My employment at the Bureau is almost at an end. I have three months to figure out what the future holds. But whenever I think of what it might look like, I still see her in it.

She answers with a wary, "Agent Knox?"

"Yes, ma'am."

"Is everything okay?"

"Yes. Well, mostly."

"Define mostly."

"Two people broke into my house last night while I was sleeping."

"How many of them are dead?"

"Neither."

"Well, I have to say, I'm not sure whether to be relieved or disappointed."

"I'm feeling a bit of both myself."

"I'm going with relieved. I think." I smile to myself, realizing how much I'm going to miss her. She clears her throat. The tinge of humor in her voice is gone when she asks, "Are we thinking this was a random occurrence? Or…"

Though she doesn't say it, I know what she's asking. It's the reason why I first came back here in the first place. The reason why my grandfather was murdered, a conspiracy so deep that if it had a bottom, neither of us got close enough to see it.

"I don't think it's connected," I say slowly, deliberately choosing my words.

"But?"

"But I don't think it was entirely random, either."

I stand in Butch's bedroom doorway, staring inside. Besides the broken glass from the window I shot out that litters the carpet, there's nothing else in there besides the box of keepsakes that I'd found in his closet.

"Then why were they there? What were they after?"

Crossing the room, I look down at the box. The lid is still on. It doesn't appear to have been disturbed. But when I'd first spotted the perp, they'd been on their knees, very close to it. What had they been doing?

"I'm not sure," I say.

One thing is clear, though. They'd come straight through the house to Butch's bedroom. Whatever they wanted, they thought they'd find it in here.

"You're good, though?" she asks.

"Yeah. I just thought I should let you know what happened."

"I appreciate that. Also, if you find anything out?"

"I'll keep you updated."

"Please do. And Cassidy?"

"Yes?"

"Stay safe."

Though I agree before ending the call, something tells me that's going to be hard to do. Whatever they were after, they wanted it badly enough to break in when they knew I was home. And something tells me that despite the not-so-friendly greeting I gave them, they won't hesitate to return, no matter how unwise that would seem.

CHAPTER 4

My throat is tight. And my chest. My jaw and the rest of my muscles are too. Let's face it—my entire body is tied in knots. Fear and anger have collided and twisted me into a mangled mess. My teeth ache from clenching, and a dull headache throbs behind my eyes.

And yet, slowly, by degrees, the tension that consumes me relaxes its iron grip. There's something about being here, at the sanctuary. Something about the familiar scents of the barn that takes me back to my childhood, to a time when I felt safe and secure. Something about the warmth of the bodies in the stalls around me, the gentle eyes that look back at me, that soothes my soul.

Or, in the case of the baby zebra in the stall before me, mischievous ones. Her mother nickers softly as I put some hay in her net. Braces her feet against her foal's assault as the little one knocks against her while I watch. A sense of calm envelops me.

It's a blessing—today of all days, I need to relax. Even if I hadn't been woken in the middle of the night by a pair of home invaders, I'd be nervous. In a few hours, I get to pick up Jake from the hospital and bring him home.

My heart gives a strange little flutter, equal parts excited and terrified. Tonight, I could find myself in his arms. Or alone on my couch, broken hearted. Because as much as I want him in my life, he's a smart man—he shouldn't want to be in mine.

I've already almost gotten him killed once. He might not be so lucky the next time. And though I try not to think about what might have happened if he'd been here during the break-in last night, I can't help but fear how it would have ended.

Stephano *baas* at my feet as if to assure me I should stay positive. I stop what I'm doing for a minute, giving him my full attention. Can't help smiling as he performs a series of hops, dancing at my feet. He's not the first goat to ever call the sanctuary home, but he's certainly the most charming and by far the cutest.

He turns his tiny pygmy face up to me and sticks his tongue out. It's accompanied by a sound that can best be described as belonging to a dinosaur. It's not part of his repertoire. I turn, spotting Flap, a pelican missing half a wing, as he waddles into the barn.

"Hungry?" I ask.

He eyes me in that strange way fowl have, that primal look that says they remember the time when they ruled the Earth. When humans would have been on the menu, instead of leaving fishing line in the water to get wrapped around a young bird's wing. If I didn't already have enough reasons to distrust my fellow man, that right there would do the trick.

He, Stephano, and the zebras are just a few of the rescues that call the Gator Glade Sanctuary home. Animals who have been injured, abandoned, neglected, abused, or are in want of a safe place to live out the rest of their days.

My grandfather, Butch, created this place deep in the heart of the Florida Everglades to fill a need. I just don't think he ever expected that need to be inside his granddaughter's chest.

Or maybe he had. Butch had an almost preternatural ability to predict things like that, especially where I was concerned. In a life defined by loss, his hit me harder than I ever could have anticipated. It left me truly alone in this world until I reconnected with Jake. I came too close to being that way again when he got shot.

My tension returns swiftly and with a vengeance. I hurry into the tack room, cross to the refrigerator and pull out a fish. Toss it to Flap. The bird catches the snack in his oversized beak and gulps it down. I give him another, slop the pigs, split a banana between them and give the peel to Stephano.

The tiny goat bobs his head as he chews his favorite treat. For the moment, everyone here is satisfied—except me. Because all the fears I've been trying so hard to ignore are back at the forefront of my mind.

Last night's break in is just the latest in a series of disasters to plague me. If there's one thing I've learned from my past, it's that people aren't safe around me. And now the time has come to face the consequences of that.

CHAPTER 5

Each beat of my heart makes me feel a little more nervous. Because each beat means this trip is a little closer to the end. And I don't think I'm ready for that just yet.

There are too many unknowns. Too many possibilities. Too many things outside of my control.

I tell myself to relax, but I'm not sure that I can. Though I try to be discreet as I glance at the man in the passenger seat beside me, I fail. Our eyes meet, locking in a way that's dangerous while driving. But that's not the only threat.

Swallowing hard, I return my focus to the road. I can still feel him looking at me, my skin hot where his gaze is, my palms sweaty on the wheel. And that smile he's giving me? It's a good thing I'm sitting right now, because it makes my knees weak.

Jake Walker was my first friend. My best friend until my parents died and his mom took off, leaving him with his abusive father. Then, when we crossed paths again in high school, he became my first crush.

Life intervened, and I left our hometown of Gator Glade, but when I returned for Butch's funeral after having been away for twenty years, the spark was still there—and mutual. Things were starting to heat up, when he claimed another first. The first man to get shot for me.

I'm not quite sure where we stand now, but since we're driving away from the hospital, alone for the first time in almost a week, I expect I'm going to find out soon. As the road narrows to the single eastbound lane that will lead us into the swamp, he releases a heavy sigh.

"You sound relieved," I say.

"I am. There's no way I would have survived another day in there."

"It couldn't have been that bad."

"Don't get me wrong. Being served all those meals in bed was nice. You definitely won't hear any complaints from me if you decide you want to keep that going."

I roll my eyes even though I feel a secret thrill that he's referenced a future with me in it. I'd been so worried that he'd be ready to run from my life now that he's had a chance to think about it.

"But if I was there any longer, I'd have turned to mush."

Not likely. I checked him out plenty in that thin hospital gown he was wearing, and his muscles look in fine form. My cheeks flush as I think exactly how fine.

"I wouldn't have thought I'd have missed mucking stalls and hauling bales of hay so much, but I can't wait to get back at it."

"Uh, no," I say, frowning at the road in front of me. "That's not happening."

"Why not?"

"Didn't you hear anything the doctor went over when she was discharging you? You're supposed to keep your arm in the sling and immobile for at least the next two weeks, until your check-up."

"She didn't mean it."

"I'm pretty sure she did."

"Trust me, she didn't. They just have to say that stuff to cover themselves for insurance purposes."

"Do I need to turn this car around and go back so we can ask her?"

I tighten my hands on the wheel so he knows I'm serious about carrying out the threat as I look at him, only to find him grinning at me. I can't tell if he's teasing or not, though I suspect not. Which means I'll have to find a way to keep him distracted if he decides to try going rogue.

Though I feel a flash of heat as I think of different ways I might do that, it gets doused like a bucket of ice water just got dumped over my head a moment later. I swallow hard as I think about the wound still healing on my back, the brand put there by a serial killer. The one I've yet to tell Jake about, a secret I feel strangely desperate to keep concealed from him.

How long can I keep my shirt on—both metaphorically and literally? Long enough for the scar to not look so angry and inflamed? To have it covered with a tattoo so Jake never has to know it's there? Until I come to terms with the shame of what was done to me? What if that never happens?

"How's the crew been doing?" he asks, interrupting my thoughts as the driveway appears ahead. "Daisy and Charlie? Stephano?"

"Fine," I say, easing off the gas. "You can see for yourself in just a second."

Jake's seatbelt clicks as I make the turn. He shifts to face me. "That's going to have to wait."

His voice has gone deep and husky. My pulse jumps into overdrive, my worries of a moment ago battling a desire just as strong. I resist the urge to race down the dirt road to the house, worried the pits and bumps will jar his injured shoulder.

He's out of the car before I've even put it in park. I hurry to kill the engine and unbuckle my seatbelt as he rounds the front of the vehicle. A second later, my door opens. He extends his hand to me. I take it, allowing him to pull me from the vehicle, straight into his embrace.

Our lips meet, his good arm tightening around me, pinning me to him as he walks backward, toward the door. I fumble blindly for my keys as we reach the threshold, give up the battle, letting them drop so I can wrap my arms around his neck instead. It's only after we're both breathless that the kiss ends, his forehead tipped against mine while we stare into each other's eyes, grinning goofily.

"It feels like I've been waiting forever to do that," he says.

"It was a good practice round," I admit.

"Once we're inside, we'll see if I can do better."

I release him reluctantly and grab my keys from the dirt at our feet. Sort through them for the right one. When I look back up, it's to find him frowning.

"What's the matter?"

"What happened here?" he asks, tapping the cardboard I taped over the broken windowpane.

"It broke. It's no big deal. We already have new doors on order, remember?"

But something in my expression must give me away.

"Cassie, how long has it been like this?"

Sighing, I say, "Since last night." I look away, busying myself with fitting the key in the lock as I add, "There was a break-in."

"Why didn't you tell me?"

"I didn't want you to worry."

"Well, I am worried. You should be too. Do you think it has anything to do with what happened to Butch?"

"No."

Walking inside, I hang my purse on the coatrack by the door, though it's an awful place to keep it, all things considered. Jake follows close at my heels, the conversation not done.

"How can you be so sure?"

"Because people like that wouldn't have bothered with a little breaking and entering. They would have just burned the house down while I slept, made it look like an electrical fire or something."

"You were here when it happened?" He curses. "That's it. You're staying at my place."

"I can't leave the animals here by themselves."

"Then I'll stay here. I'll sleep on the couch."

"No. Jake, it's fine. You need to sleep in a bed so you can heal."

He was the one who got hurt last time. The last thing I want is for him to be the first line of defense. I don't need a human shield.

"I'll heal just fine regardless." He reaches out, his hand brushing against my cheek. "I'm not going anywhere."

But maybe he should. He almost lost his life because of me. Next time he might not be so lucky.

Not for the first time I wonder if I shouldn't put an end to whatever this is that's happening between us to keep him safe. But I'm too selfish for that. Too weak. I'm not sure I've ever wanted anything as much as I want him in my life, and it's absolutely terrifying.

"Fine. But I'm sleeping on the couch."

"It'll be a tight squeeze, but I'm game," he grins.

I stare at the ceiling as I shake my head, sighing, but any annoyance I feel vanishes as his arms wrap around me. His head lowers toward mine. My breath catches as he stops just before our lips make contact. "Seriously,

Cassie. I can't lose you. Promise me you'll be careful."

I want to beg the same of him. To explain that I might not survive if anything happens to him, especially if it's my fault. I already have my partner's death on my hands. I'd never forgive myself if I had his, as well.

Before I can utter the words, a thunderous crash rips through the air around us. The windows rattle in their frames. And even before the echo of the noise has faded, Jake's on the move, yelling for me to stay where I am while he runs outside.

CHAPTER 6

I don't know what I've ever done to give that man the impression that I'm the type to take orders, but he's mistaken. Cursing, I follow him, wishing he'd taken a moment to think things through before bolting to see what happened. It's probably something harmless.

But what if it's not?

A cloud of dust rises behind Jake as he races toward the barn. And I admit, since the source of the bang isn't obviously apparent at first glance, that seems the likeliest source. But on second glance, the animals in the paddock—Hildegarde, the cow; Daisy and Charlie, the zebras; Sam, the mule—aren't looking at either of us. They're looking toward the road.

This right here is why it pays to take the time to think before acting. I call out to him as I race up the driveway, not pausing to see if he follows, which is me not taking my own advice, but whatever. At least I'm heading in the right direction.

As the road comes into view, I come to a sudden stop, shocked by what I see. Pulling my cell from my pocket, I dial 911 as I force myself back into motion, hurrying toward the vehicle wrapped around a tree trunk just to the left of the driveway.

Across the road, on the far side of the guardrail, a large alligator splashes noisily into the canal at my frantic approach. My heart beats wildly in my chest. My lungs ache with exertion, emotion, the stench of burned rubber as I tell the emergency dispatcher what's happened, and where.

I scan the earth beneath the car as I get closer, checking for leaking gasoline, but the ground is cast in shadow—if there's liquid seeping from the vehicle, I can't see it. Despite that, the hair on my arms rises, the danger of the situation felt on a primal level as I get close enough to see through the shattered window and catch my first glimpse of the occupant inside.

The steering wheel has been shoved into the driver's chest by the force of the impact. Their face is covered in blood. Long hair and slender hands are my only clues that it's a woman.

Swallowing down the fear blocking my throat, I grab the door handle and try to open it. It won't budge.

I barely register the sound of Jake's steps as he comes up behind me. Nor the touch of his hand as it lands on my shoulder. I give him a desperate look as I update the dispatcher, "The driver's door won't open. We'll need fire rescue to cut her out."

As I step back, Jake takes my place, pulling at the door as I round to the other side of the vehicle. But as I reach the rear, I stop. The back right of the truck is crushed at an angle.

This wasn't an accident. Someone purposely sent this woman into the tree.

Forensics may be able to eventually tell us who did this, but why? That's a secret only the woman and her assailant can tell. So let's hope that she's able to.

I continue on my journey, opening the passenger door with trembling hands. For some reason, knowing this was intentional makes what I'm about to do feel even more hazardous. As if to second the thought, Jake says my name in a low warning tone.

But I ignore everything—him, the feeling, the tinny voice of the emergency dispatcher as I set my phone onto the dash, freeing both my hands. Then, carefully, I climb inside.

As I do, the woman's eyes flutter. A surge of hope propels me closer.

"It's going to be okay," I assure her. "Can you tell me your name?"

The woman doesn't speak, possibly can't. But the sound of my voice seems to be bringing her around, so I continue.

"My name is Cassidy, but my friends call me Cassie."

By friends, I mean Jake. When we were little, that middle syllable was a challenge, so he dropped it. This time, when the woman's eyes flutter, they fix on me.

"We're going to get you out of here, okay? Help is on the way."

Grabbing the hem of my shirt, I rip a strip off, using the material to gently wipe blood from around the woman's eyes. But some of the blood has dried already, forming a thick crust beneath the fresh. Strange.

Other than a small split in the skin beneath her eyebrow that's slowly weeping, I don't see any other facial lacerations. Certainly nothing that would account for so much blood so fast.

But maybe the injury didn't happen during the accident. Maybe it happened before. And maybe it was caused by whoever drove her into this tree.

"You're safe now," I whisper, tucking a strand of blood-soaked hair behind her ear. As my hand drops, she grabs it. The look in her eyes as they meet mine reveals everything I need to know—she doesn't believe what I've said.

"Who hurt you?" I ask, raising my voice to be heard over the approaching sirens, a chill spreading across my skin despite the stifling heat inside the vehicle. "Can you tell me?"

But she never gets the chance. Chaos ensues as a team of firefighters and paramedics descend on us.

"Ma'am, we need you to exit the vehicle," one tells me, but the woman refuses to release my hand. I give them an apologetic look. Climb onto the middle console to give them room to enter behind me and squeeze myself as small as I can as they work to stabilize her.

Even after they have her head immobilized, and her door cut away, she doesn't let go. So I climb across the car to maintain the physical connection between us as they remove her and strap her to a gurney. And though they don't want to let me in the ambulance, they don't have a choice.

Whatever happened to this woman, it's left her terrified. There's no way I'm turning my back on her now.

CHAPTER 7

The drive to the hospital is intense, partly because it's a reminder of a similar journey I made with Jake less than a week ago, but mostly because there's so much going on. The paramedic is in constant motion, taking stock of the woman's injuries, checking her vitals, asking her questions—none of which she answers.

And the longer I spend time with her, looking into her eyes, the more it becomes clear. It's not because she can't. It's because she won't. This woman is afraid to say a word, even if it's at the expense of her own health.

But that's not the only thing that's bothering me. There's something familiar about her. I don't recognize her, and yet, I can't shake the feeling that we've met before. The fact that she clings to my hand like it's the only thing keeping her tethered to this Earth helps cement this notion.

Or maybe I'm reading too much into it. Traumatic events are known for creating fast bonds between strangers. And it's possible that what I recognize is my own fear mirrored back at me.

Before I can decide, we reach our destination. The back doors to the ambulance swing open suddenly, and she's forced to release my hand as the gurney is pulled from the vehicle. A horde of doctors and nurses descend, gathering around her, accessing her condition as they wheel her inside.

"Ma'am, you can't go in there," one of them tells me as I move to follow. "Someone will come find you in the waiting room and give you an update once we know what we're dealing with."

I cast a desperate look at the woman. Her terrified eyes meet mine between the shoulders of the medical staff tending to her. But there's nothing I can do. I watch helplessly as the doors close behind her. Then I hurry around the outside of the building to the waiting room entrance.

Jake's already there when I arrive, his face collapsing with relief when he sees me. He closes the distance between us in two giant steps, his hands taking me gently by the shoulders, holding me in place while he inspects me.

"Are you okay?" he asks.

"Yeah."

He releases a heavy sigh. "So none of that's yours?"

I follow his gaze, noticing for the first time the red stains that cover my clothes and hands.

"No."

He mutters a prayer of thanks, dropping a kiss onto the crown of my head as he draws me into a hug. I burrow against him. Squeeze my eyes shut, trying to erase the fear I'd seen in the woman's expression, the emotion so palpable that I can still feel it clinging to my skin.

Much like her blood. I rub my fingers together behind Jake's back. Though the blood on them has dried, it's still tacky. But when I'd wiped the fresh blood from the woman's face, the dried blood underneath had been flaky.

How had that happened? How much time would that take?

I try to calculate how long I've had her blood on me. The drive from the sanctuary to the hospital would normally take thirty-five minutes. In a speeding ambulance, the travel time's probably cut by a third.

But then there was how long it took the ambulance to respond, and for fire rescue to cut her out of the ruined vehicle. A conservative estimate for how long her blood's been on my hands would be forty minutes, though it's possibly closer to an hour.

She could have driven from Miami in that time. Or from any of the dozens of places along the way. For all I know, she'd come from the neighbor's house, though I doubt old Mrs. Baker was the one to cause her injuries.

There's no telling where she was hurt, or by who. But I suspect that if I can get her alone, she'll tell me.

"I don't suppose it would do me any good if I asked you not to do something like that again, would it?" Jake asks.

"Like what?" My words are muffled against his chest.

"Like getting in a wrecked vehicle. Putting yourself at risk."

I open my mouth to argue. Close it. Tighten my arms around him, a lump growing in my throat as I realize how I would have felt if our roles had been reversed—if I'd been the one to watch him climb into a ruin of twisted metal.

"Probably not. But if it helps any, I'm sorry."

He sighs, pulling back so I can see his exasperation. The stern look he gives me quickly softens. "What am I going to do with you?"

I try to think of an answer that will lighten the mood, but before I can, a question comes from behind me.

"You're the one who came in with the auto accident victim, right?"

Jake releases me so I can turn to face the nurse. "I am. Is she okay? When can I see her?"

"Tomorrow at the soonest."

"Tomorrow?"

"She's heading into surgery now. If she's out tonight, she won't be allowed any visitors. Even tomorrow you'll probably want to call first." The nurse gives me a sympathetic smile. "I'm sorry, I know it's not what you wanted to hear. But we'll take good care of her, I promise."

I nod, swallowing down my disappointment.

"I don't suppose you could help us with her paperwork? She doesn't have any identification on her."

"I'm sorry, I can't. I'm afraid I don't even know her name. I just found her after the crash."

"Oh." She gives me an odd look. One that suggests I'm strange for desperately wanting to see a stranger. "Then you'll definitely want to call first. Only immediate family will be allowed to visit while she's on the trauma unit. Given the extent of her injuries, she might be there for a few days, maybe more."

The idea of waiting that long for answers makes my stomach churn, but what can I do?

"Were the two of you involved in the accident?" she asks. "Do either of you need medical attention?"

Her question takes me off guard. I know I look like I've been part of a crime scene, but Jake never entered the vehicle with her. I turn to look at him behind me, my heart skipping a beat when I see the bright red bloom on the front of his shirt. I'd been so wrapped up in the mystery of what happened to the woman that I hadn't even noticed.

And neither, apparently, had he. He stares down at the blood, frowning.

"You must have torn your stitches," I say.

Turning to the nurse, I explain, "He was just discharged this morning after surgery to repair a gunshot wound." When her eyebrows arch, I add, "He was injured in a home invasion."

It's not quite the truth, but an abbreviated and possibly more believable version than what really happened.

"Who was his physician?"

"Dr. Perez."

"Come on. I'll check if she can see you. If not, we'll get someone else to take a look."

I grab Jake's hand as she leads us to the back. Hold it tight as she gets him settled on a bed before going to get the doctor, feeling horrible.

"Cassie," he says.

"What?"

"Stop."

I give him a questioning look.

"I can tell that you're trying to blame yourself. It's not your fault."

How can I explain to him that I'm afraid that it might be? That this is what's in store for him if he's a part of my life? It seems only fair to warn him. To make sure he knows what he's getting into.

"Back so soon?" Dr. Perez pulls the curtain along the rail surrounding the bed for privacy as she enters. She eyes the blood on Jake's shirt before giving him a stern look. "We have to stop meeting like this, Mr. Walker. What happened?"

"I'm not sure."

She turns her gaze to me.

"There was an accident. A woman crashed her car into a tree. I can only guess that he tore his stitches trying to pull her door open."

"Well, I suppose I can't fault you too much for that.

Let's see what the damage is. Shirt off."

I look away as Jake releases my hand to undress. Flinch as he hisses while the doctor inspects his wound. When she's done, she sighs heavily.

"You've torn a couple of your internal sutures," she says. "Considering they were there in the first place to hold the ends of your muscle in place while it mended, it's not ideal."

"So now what?" Jake asks.

"How do you feel about having permanent damage to your shoulder?"

"Not great."

"Then you're going to have to take it easy. I'm serious. Arm in the sling for three weeks."

"Three? What happened to two?"

"Two was when the sutures were in place. Opening the wound back up to replace them at this point would just undo the healing that's already occurred, so we're not going to do that. Instead, you're going to avoid all physical activity—including being intimate—until your next checkup. You'll have to call my office to reschedule for a later date."

My cheeks are already burning, but when both the doctor and Jake turn to stare at me as if I'm the one solely in control of all this, it's a miracle I don't burst into flames.

"I'm serious," she says, still looking at me. Then, turning to him, "If you keep disrupting the healing process, you're risking a permanent loss of strength, range of motion, and ability. So do us all a favor, Mr. Walker, and behave yourself."

She says that like it's easy. And maybe in her world, it is. But now that Jake's a part of my life, I have serious concerns. Because my reality? It's messy and unruly and has a really bad habit of being dangerous.

CHAPTER 8

Though I thought it would be smarter for me to wait in the car, Jake insists that I come in when we stop by his condo for him to grab some clothes on the way back to my house. And though I figured it would be awkward given the ban on getting too affectionate with each other, that's not why I find myself so uncomfortable right now.

His place is nothing like I expected. It's like entering another world. As a partner at one of the swankiest corporate law firms in Florida, I knew he made a lot of money, but I'm only beginning to realize what that means.

To start, the two doormen didn't even blink when they greeted us as we walked by, despite the fact that we both look like we've walked off the set of a horror movie. It makes me wonder what other kinds of things they're used to turning a blind eye to. How much they get paid not to see what's right in front of them.

Then there's his unit itself. My apartment in Virginia is nice, but the wide-open space and high-end fixtures I see when we walk inside Jake's place make mine look downright shabby. Not to mention his luxurious furnishings, a shock considering that when I first came back down here, I'd found him camping out in a tent in the sanctuary's barn.

It's nothing like I would have expected, and that

makes me nervous. Is this just for show, or have I only seen what I wanted to, without taking a close enough look at the man I'm falling for? Have I made a mistake by assuming I know him just because that was once true?

It makes me wonder what else I haven't noticed about Jake.

Though he tells me to make myself at home, I linger by the door, aware of how filthy I am. Not wanting to make a mess and get his pristine space dirty. Because the blood that's on me? It's finally flaking off.

I'm staring out the window at the view, impressive even from where I stand across the room, when he comes back, a duffel bag slung over his good shoulder, a pillow pinned under his sling.

"Need some help?" I ask, eyeing the bag which looks stuffed full to the seams. How long is he planning on staying? I decide I don't care.

"Nope." He drops the bag on the floor and sets the pillow on top. "You want a drink?"

"I'm good, thanks."

"A snack?"

I shake my head. Yet still he comes closer, until he's standing right in front of me.

"It's okay to step away from the door, you know."

"Another time. I don't want to get anything dirty."

"I don't mind."

"But I do."

"I want you to be comfortable here."

His hand caresses my cheek. He presses his lips against mine. But as much as I long to lose myself in it, to block out the memory of what happened earlier today, last night, the previous week, this entire past month from hell, while I'm at it, to silence the noise inside my head, I stop him as it grows more passionate.

"You heard what the doctor said," I remind him.

"What doctor?" he asks, giving me a wicked grin.

"You'd make a horrible politician."

"I'm pretty sure I just met the requirement for being a great one." He sighs dramatically, then smirks as he adds, "It's for the best, anyway."

Suddenly suspicious, I ask, "And why's that?"

"Because I don't want our kid to think I gave it up too soon."

"Our kid?" I try to play it cool, but on the inside, I'm reeling. Because even if I wasn't almost forty, and we hadn't *just* reconnected, I'm in nowhere near the right kind of headspace to even consider bringing a child into this world.

I glance away, searching for a reflective surface, sure that my expression has betrayed me. When I look back, his eyes are full of amusement. He gives me a wicked grin.

"Yeah. Stephano."

My heart feels like a water balloon squeezed just shy of bursting as I suck in a relieved breath. That was mean. I'll definitely find a way to pay him back for that.

"You discuss our sex life with the goat?"

"Well, I haven't yet. It's just that when I do, I don't want him to judge me. I want to be respectable."

"Which means what, exactly?"

"That we should probably wait the standard three dates."

"Just three?"

"You're right. We can do better. How about four?"

"Or six," I suggest.

"Okay, then. Six it is. Actual dates. Involving going out in public."

"Yes," I agree. "And each date has to be on its own day."

"Okay."

"And they have to be spaced out. At least seventy-two hours in between."

Jake's mouth drops open. I watch him doing the math, spot the moment he realizes that would bring us to the three-week recheck with his doctor. Revenge achieved, this time, I'm the one to grin. Trying not to gloat, I step by him and grab his pillow, then snatch his bag from the floor, slinging it over my shoulder.

"What?" I make my best innocent face, though it's hard not to laugh at his shocked expression. All he can do is shake his head.

Putting a hand on his chest to steady myself, I rise up on my toes until my lips are almost touching his. "I don't want to have to tell the kid that when you finally gave it up, I damaged you." Lowering back down, I gesture with my head toward the door, "Come on, we've got to get back. Right about now, that goat's probably getting hungry."

As I lead the way out the door, I hear him mumbling something about me not playing fair. It puts a huge smile on my face, even before he catches up, falling into step beside me on the way to the elevator.

"Oh, it's on," he says.

"It is," I agree. "But not a moment too soon."

There's only one problem with that. With him staying at my place, it's going to be hard to stick to my own rules. For once, the brand on my back serves a purpose other than as a constant, painful reminder of what happens when I let my guard down.

CHAPTER 9

My stomach lurches when we return to the sanctuary and spot Sheriff Kingston's cruiser parked on the side of the road just outside the driveway. Two encounters with the man in less than twenty-four hours seems like more than anyone should have to bear.

But as Jake slows to make the turn and the man himself steps out of the shade, blocking our path with his arms crossed, it's clear that's exactly what I'm going to have to do.

"I'll deal with this. Why don't you go ahead on to the house and get settled," I say.

Jake gives me a doubtful look. "You sure?"

"Yeah. It'll go quicker if there's only one of us here for him to insult."

I hop out before he has a chance to reply. Walk over to the site of the crash, hoping Kingston will follow.

Though the truck has been removed and the scraps of the wreck swept away, what happened here today will be evident for years to come—perhaps even decades. I stare at the deep scar gouged into the tree. The tiny shards of safety glass glittering in the churned-up soil. The lack of tire marks on the road.

"Prime example of why you shouldn't drink and drive right here," Sheriff Kingston says, coming up behind me.

I turn to face him. "What makes you think she'd been drinking?"

"You got a better reason for why someone would lose control of their car and slam it into a tree?"

"She didn't lose control."

"You think it was on purpose, then?"

"I don't."

"What other explanation is there?"

"Didn't you notice the huge dent on the right rear of the vehicle?"

"Yeah. So?"

"I think someone intentionally ran her into the tree."

He gives me a doubtful look. "Why would someone do that?"

"I'm not sure yet. But I saw that woman, Sheriff. Climbed into the truck with her while we were waiting for the ambulance. Held her hand the entire way to the hospital. She wasn't drunk."

"I imagine a crash like that would sober you right up."

"I couldn't smell any alcohol on her. I don't think she'd been drinking."

"But you can't say for sure."

"No. But what I can say is that the woman was terrified."

"Well, of course she was. She tried to saw a tree in half with her car."

I shake my head in frustration. It would be easier if the person who's supposed to be investigating the accident was looking in the right direction. But maybe that's too much to ask for.

"Forty-some years of law enforcement has taught me that the simplest explanation is usually the right one. You ask me, that dent was probably on the vehicle before today. She's probably got a history of drunk driving."

"You run the VIN?" I ask, inquiring about the vehicle identification number all vehicles have.

"I tried. It's been ground off. No registration papers in the glove box, either. And the tag came back as reported stolen."

Something shifts inside me. The tiny voice that's been whispering that something was off about the accident has turned into a yell.

"And in your forty-plus years of experience, you ever have a drunk driver go to those lengths before?"

He shrugs. "There's a first time for everything. You think car thieves are above taking a nip before driving?"

My skin crawls as he takes a step closer, studying my face.

"You really believe your little knocked-into-the-tree theory, don't you? I'm going to do you a favor and ease your mind. I saw where that dent was. There's no way another vehicle struck her there to cause the accident. Not traveling west, like she was."

"What if she was in the wrong lane?"

"If she was in the wrong lane, that opens a whole new can of worms, doesn't it? Are you suggesting that maybe she was trying to pass and got hit?"

I turn to look at the road. I've been passed enough times by careless drivers myself on this stretch that it's not hard to imagine. But she was sent into that tree with more force than if she'd just been clipped because she'd tried to get back in the correct lane too soon.

But what other explanation is there? I imagine two cars racing side by side, penned in by the canal on the right, the wood line on the left. The sinking sun casts the channel across the street into shadows, but I don't have to see it to know what's there.

The darkness of the water. The prehistoric reptiles that call it home.

I recall the loud splash one had made as I'd run up to the accident, the alligator not bothered by speeding vehicles, or even the noise of the crash, only by the presence of a human. But if that human had been dead, or even just covered in blood and injured, unable to escape…

"She wasn't trying to pass," I say with complete conviction. "Someone was trying to run her off the road. She got in the eastbound lane so if they succeeded, she'd go into the trees instead of the water."

Sheriff Kingston squints as if trying to see what I do in the fading light. Finally, he shakes his head. "That's some conspiracy you got there."

"Are you saying it's not possible?"

"Anything's possible."

"Will you at least take the measurements and run them through a simulator, see if they fit? Collect any paint transfer from the dent?"

"I'll look into it. But you mark my words. When I receive the driver's blood alcohol level from the hospital? I guarantee that will be all I need to close this case, pass it off from my plate to the district attorney's."

Though I want to argue, I don't. It's getting late. The sun is setting.

Right now, my time is better spent getting all the animals fed and watered. Taking a long, hot shower. And hibernating for the next year and a half.

"In the meantime, try to lay low, huh? I swear, I've never met anyone who is such a magnet for trouble."

I bite my tongue before I can respond. What can I really say? If you look at my life lately, he's not exactly wrong.

CHAPTER 10

A wave of déjà vu sweeps over me as my eyes open. It's dark. I have the uncanny sensation of having been awoken by a noise. And that I'm not alone in the room. I'm not sure how I know just yet, other than that my senses are screaming it.

I lie still, holding my breath. My fingers tighten, curling into fists around the blanket that covers me. I search the shadows, eyes landing on the piece of cardboard taped over the broken glass pane in the door across the room.

After much negotiation, Jake and I finally reached a compromise last night. He agreed to take the bed, but only if we pulled the couch along the back wall, as far away from the entry as possible.

That's where I am now as I listen to the soft whisper of footsteps against carpet coming from the hall. Closing my eyes all but a sliver, I watch through my lashes as a man appears from the darkness. He stops at the foot of the couch, looking down at me.

I know the instant his shape comes into view that it's Jake, can tell by the familiar breadth of his shoulders, the way he holds himself, the way he moves, but still, I don't stir. I pretend to be asleep as he comes closer, straining to see as he bends toward the floor by where my phone lies. He drops a kiss silently on my forehead, his lips soft and hot against my skin. And then he's gone.

He must be leaving to go to work, though he hadn't said anything about it before. It's too soon, if you ask me. But at least he doesn't have to do anything physical while he's there. I don't think.

It reminds me of how much I don't know about who he is now and what his life is like. I reach, checking for my phone. Find it exactly where I left it, only now it sits atop a folded piece of paper that he placed beneath it.

My hand curls around both, moving them to my chest, debating. I know I should go back to sleep. I have a long day ahead of me.

But I suspect that won't be possible. Especially not until I know what he left me. Thumbing my phone on, I use the light from the screen to illuminate his note.

Heading in to work for a bit. I'll grab some takeout for dinner on my way back. Text me later. –J

I feel silly for pretending to be asleep. I should have at least said goodbye. Why didn't I? Did I just want to avoid an awkward encounter, the decision of how much affection to exchange before he left? With morning breath? Oily skin? Bedhead?

Or had there been another reason?

I trust Jake. He risked his life for me. Got shot saving me. And yet, my first impulse had been to check my phone after he left, to make sure it was still there. No wonder I'm being forced to see a shrink.

With that realization, and the fact that my first appointment with my new psychologist is later today, I'm fully awake. There's not even a chance of getting back to sleep now. Nervous energy has me fully wired, pulsing under my skin like an electrical current. Groaning, I kick off the blanket and swing my feet to the floor.

I wasn't always so neurotic. But it's also not like I

don't have good cause. Like Sheriff Kingston said, I'm a magnet for trouble. In the past thirty hours, I've been the victim of a home invasion and a woman almost died when her vehicle was sent into a tree at the entrance of my driveway.

An icy sensation travels down the length of my spine. A tightness gathers in my chest.

What are the odds? Not just the two occurrences happening so close together, although that's strange enough. But that the woman crashed into a tree so close.

Houses along this part of the Tamiami are few and far between. Most are miles apart. Of those that do exist, many—including the sanctuary—are hard to spot until you're passing by. Unless you already know they're there.

There were no brake marks on the road, no indication that the woman had been slowing down before she was hit. In fact, the force with which she struck the tree would suggest that she'd been speeding.

And yet, of all the trees that line the road, for her to have hit the one she did… It's almost like someone is trying to send me a message.

I tug on my clothes quickly, eager to get out to the barn, where I won't feel so alone. But before I leave the house, I check the surveillance cameras from the app on my phone, making sure I'm the only human on the property. And then I pull Butch's old revolver from beneath my pillow and tuck it into the back of my shorts.

Just in case. Maybe I'm overreacting, but better that than getting caught off guard.

As I head out into the predawn peace, it's hard to imagine anything bad happening here. But I know otherwise. There's always something dark lurking beneath the surface, waiting for an opportunity to strike. And I don't just mean alligators.

I'm determined not to let that happen. My grandfather dedicated his life to making this a safe place. And I'm going to do everything within my power to keep it that way.

Entering the barn, I close my eyes for a moment. Let the musky scent of the animals mixed with the sweet odor of hay and grain fill my lungs. Listen to the soft sounds as they begin to stir from their slumber.

The gentle snort of the zebra. The low of the cow. The sound of Stephano's hooves as they touch against the top of his stall door before he hops to the ground by my feet.

Scooping him up, I wait for the sense of calm that usually washes over me once I'm here. But today it doesn't come. Because there's a sinking sensation in my gut. One that keeps whispering that the break-in and the crash are somehow connected—and personal.

CHAPTER 11

It starts with a tightening of my skin. Then the hair on my arms rises. Goosebumps appear. And though I try my best to fight it, I fail. A shiver takes hold, causing my entire body to quake.

"Are you all right?"

"Yes, fine," I say, forcing a cheerful smile. Everything's fine. Or great. I haven't used fantastic yet, but I've only been here five minutes. Give me time.

It's not that I don't realize that the point of talking with a psychologist isn't to pretend that everything is perfect in your life. I understand that defeats the purpose of paying some stranger to listen to you talk and give you advice in the first place. But I can't seem to help it.

In my defense, I just met the woman. And it's not like I'm here by choice—the Bureau is requiring these sessions. So, for now, if those are the answers that come out of my mouth as I sit across from Dr. Evangeline in her too-bright, over-chilled office, I'm okay with it.

I study her as she runs her palms across the thighs of her flawless white slacks. How does she keep them so spotless?

Put me in a pair of white pants and they won't stay white for long. Am I really supposed to share my messy life and chaotic inner thoughts with this woman? How could she possibly understand me when we obviously have so little in common?

"How did you get along with your partner?"

I've got another *fine* on my lips, all ready to go, only when I open my mouth, that's not what comes out. "I didn't."

It's the first honest thing I've said besides my name since I've been here. And an awful answer to start telling the truth with.

A pair of creases form between her eyebrows. She frowns as she asks, "Is that why his death affected you so strongly?"

"No."

"Were there some unexplored feelings between you? Perhaps some sexual tension?"

I burst out with a laugh, causing her frown to deepen.

"He was married—"

"That doesn't mean that romantic feelings can't develop, especially with someone you spend so much time with, like a partner," she interrupts.

"—to a man," I say, completing my sentence.

"Oh."

She stares at me like I'm some new and interesting creature she just discovered, head cocked at a slight angle, her confusion evident as she tries to decide what species I might be. I decide to cut her a break.

"He didn't like me."

"Do you know why?"

"At first it was because we had different ideas about the way things should be done."

"And then?"

I close my eyes, looking into the past. Can see myself standing on his front step, pounding on the door like I was trying to punch a hole through it. The instant he opened it, I brushed by him, storming into his townhouse uninvited.

"You filed a complaint about me?"

Special Agent Rodney Sawyer doesn't even have the decency to look ashamed. Instead, he smirks as he admits, "Yes."

"Why?"

"It's all in the complaint. Read it."

"If you have the gall to jeopardize my career over it, at least have the guts to say it to my face."

"Fine. You're too emotional."

He gestures at me as if I'm proving his point.

"And?"

"And I shouldn't have to put up with it. It's not fair for me to have to worry if my partner's going to pull her weight in a dangerous situation. Or if we're going to need to stop and buy some Midol—"

"You misogynistic son of a—. I've always *had your back. You're the one who's hung me out to dry at every opportunity. And what you've mistaken as emotional is passion for the job. I want to save people. Get the bad guys off the street."*

"You're not realistic."

"I'm realistic enough to know that you're the one with the problem, not me. And you want to talk about dangerous situations? I guarantee you every single agent at the Bureau would rather have me working beside them than you. It's not my fault if you're too worried about whether you might be risking your chance at a promotion to do your job—"

My spine stiffens as a slow clap starts behind me.

"Thank you! Someone needs to take him down a few pegs." I spin toward the intruder, find myself facing a good-looking Black man in his thirties. At first, I think they're brothers. Right up until he says, "I apologize for my husband. He thinks complaining should be an

Olympic sport. Rodney, you lied. She's not horrible at all. She's fantastic and I love her already."

I shake the memory away and answer Dr. Evangeline's question. "And then it was because I became friends with his husband. Best friends."

"How has what happened affected your friendship?"

"We haven't talked since. He won't answer my calls. He can't even stand to look at me."

"Then that's why your partner's death hit you so hard. Because you lost your closest friend."

"No." I pause a moment. As much as I don't want to tell her the answer that she's after, I find that I need to. Like a bad taste, I want it off my tongue. "It's because it was my fault."

"Why do you feel that way?"

"Aren't the details in my file?"

"I'd rather hear it from you."

I suspect she knows exactly what she's asking of me—to relive a nightmare. Waking up in the pitch black on the dirt floor of a serial killer's basement, my hands cuffed behind my back, looped around a metal support pole. Forcing myself to stay in the exact position I woke in for countless hours, biding my time.

Letting that monster think I was still passed out when he came to check on me, waiting until he got close enough, then striking out, kicking his feet out from under him. Then, when he was down, driving my heel into his throat over and over again until only one of us was still breathing.

Pulling him to me with my legs, fear almost blinding me as I worried about what would happen to me if the handcuff key wasn't in one of his pockets. The overwhelming relief I felt when I found it and unlocked the cuffs.

Blowing out a deep breath, I say, "Because after I

got free, I didn't leave quickly enough. I know that most people would have run the instant they were able to, but I just sat there. Catching my breath. And I was looking for my shirt. That's why I was still in the basement when my partner came in the house and hit the booby trap, taking a fatal shotgun blast to the chest."

"That's right. You were… injured."

It's a kind way of saying that a serial killer put his mark on me. Because that's the truth of what happened. He branded me like I was livestock. To him, I guess I was. But the shame I feel? It's pure human. And my failure to tell Jake that I have reasons of my own to want to wait to be with him other than following his doctor's orders is sheer cowardice.

"Does it hurt?" Dr. Evangeline asks.

"No," I lie.

Only when I'm not distracted. Every time I sit with my back against a chair or couch cushion or car seat. Or when I lie flat. Every time I have a moment to think. Every time I remember.

"I understand that you're originally from the area, but you've been up north for the last two decades."

"Yes. I came back when my grandfather died."

"What kind of support system do you have?"

"There or here?"

"Both."

I think of Director Jacobson and Mallory Chan. A handful of coworkers I occasionally grabbed a drink with. But since Quinten turned his back on me after Rodney died, there's no one from my old life who truly gets it. Gets me.

"I've reconnected with an old friend down here," I say.

Something in my tone must give me away, because she asks, "Romantically?"

When I don't answer, she gives me a sharp look. "Do you think that's wise? You have an awful lot going on to complicate things like that. Maybe you should hold off before rushing into anything. Just a suggestion, but I want you to think about it."

I push the same fake smile on my face that I started the session with as I stand to leave. "Thank you. I'll do that."

Dr. Evangeline glances at her watch, startled. "Oh, I hadn't realized it had gotten so late. I have a little more time if you'd like to continue?"

"I appreciate the offer, but I have another appointment to get to."

"Then we'll pick up where we left off next time."

I force myself to take careful, measured steps on the way out, fighting the urge to run. Because sharing the way I just did? Exposing my secrets? It hurts way worse than the damaged skin on my back. It feels like my wounds have been reopened. Not just the physical ones, but the mental ones, too.

CHAPTER 12

Everything feels dangerous. Life. The world. Me. Needless to say, I'm on edge as I leave the doctor's office. What was supposed to bring comfort has instead been a painful reminder of my past mistakes—and their deadly consequences.

On some level, I realize it's not my fault that I ended up in that basement. Or that my partner is dead. But even though I've managed to collect the pieces of myself and put them back together, I'm still not the woman I was before.

My confidence has been shaken, leaving me feeling rattled and off balance, like a heavy wind could blow me over. I seem to have moved beyond the panic attacks that plagued me during the first couple of weeks after my escape, but I still feel weak.

It's not something I'm used to. Or enjoy.

I was always so sure of myself and my abilities. Even as a child I knew I could take care of myself. Now? Jake got shot saving me from my grandfather's killer because I let my guard down and didn't see what was right in front of me. I made a horrible error in judgment that could have gotten me, or worse, Jake, killed.

And I can't shake the feeling that there's something important that I'm missing. That I'm at risk of making the same mistakes all over again.

Getting in my car, I start the engine and blast the AC to cool off the sweltering interior. Stare out the windshield, reluctant to move. What I need is to be able to trust myself again. But to do that, I need to figure out if the uneasy feeling in my gut whispering danger is caused by instinct, or imagination.

For over a decade of my time with the FBI, I worked as an analyst. My job was to look at the results that were spit out by a computer program used to troll the hundreds of thousands of cases reported by various law enforcement agencies across the country each year. The algorithm detected possible relationships between crimes. And I looked for patterns to establish whether a real link existed.

I wasn't just good at the job. I excelled at it.

As crazy as it might seem, I think there's a connection between the car accident yesterday and the reason someone broke into my house. That's why my nerves are on such high alert.

I need to speak with the woman. She's the only one who can confirm my suspicions. I think something bad happened to her—something other than the wreck. And for some reason, I can't shake the feeling that she was on her way to see me.

Ten minutes later, after being repeatedly transferred and placed on hold, I restate the same line I've already said half a dozen times. "Yes, I need to speak with someone about a woman who was brought in yesterday after a car accident."

"Our Jane Doe?"

My pulse quickens. "Yes."

"Are you able to identify her?"

"No. I'm the one who found her."

"Oh. I'm afraid I can't give out information to anyone who's not family."

"Would I be allowed to visit her?"

"Once she's allowed to have visitors, yes."

"Can you tell me when that might be?"

"Hopefully soon, dear. We're still waiting for her doctor to conduct a post-op check and give the go-ahead to transfer her from the trauma unit. But these things take time. I doubt it will happen before visiting hours end today."

I might go insane if I don't get some answers soon, because the fact is, I'm struggling. I don't like feeling scared, or vulnerable, or unprepared, but I'm all those things. I've been trying so hard to pretend like I've moved on from what happened in that basement. To use my lack of panic attacks as proof that everything is okay.

But it's not. I'm not.

It's possible that the break-in was just bad luck. And that the accident was only a coincidence. But sitting in therapy for the last hour made me realize something.

I've always known that I'm the type of person who needs answers. It's what made me so good at my job. But apparently, I need them so badly that it makes me do incredibly stupid things, like knock on the door of someone who I suspect is a serial killer.

My partner was right. I'm too emotional. Too impulsive.

I'm not sure I can trust myself to make rational decisions. I'm afraid I'm going to do something to get myself, or worse, Jake, hurt again. I'm desperate not to do that. I have to keep us safe. My gaze drifts from the pylon sign advertising the shops in the strip mall next door to one store in particular.

"Is there a number I can call to reach this desk directly?" I ask.

I grab a pen from the cup holder and scribble on the back of a gas receipt. Debate the wisdom of what I'm thinking as the call ends. But the decision's already been made. Turning off the car, I exit the vehicle and squeeze between two bushes in the hedge that separates the doctor's office from the parking lot next door.

A bell dings as I push my way inside. But even without the noise announcing my arrival, I suspect I would still draw attention. That tends to happen when you're the only woman in a place. Scanning the room quickly, I locate what I want and approach the counter.

"May I help you, ma'am?"

I give the clerk, a man in his fifties with thick glasses and a kind face, a smile and point at the wall behind him.

"Yes. To start, I'd like that Mossberg pump action shotgun."

He looks over his shoulder at the weapon I've indicated, then turns back to face me.

"Have you ever used a gun like that before, ma'am?"

Only in training, though I don't say that.

"I have. I'd also like that compact SIG Sauer P229 you have in the case. And I'll need a .45, if you can point me in the right direction."

Leaning over the counter closer to me, he asks in a low voice, "Are you in some kind of trouble, dear?"

I'd like to know the answer to that question myself. But even if I'm not, I should have a firearm besides Butch's old revolver. And since my service weapons are still in an evidence box in Virginia, I don't see what choice I have other than to buy new ones.

I brighten my smile, pretending that this is the most natural thing in the world. "No, sir. Just doing a little retail therapy."

"When my wife buys this fast and furious, it's usually at a shoe store."

Shrugging, I say, "Shoes aren't really my thing."

"You realize there's going to be a three-day wait, don't you?"

Reaching into my purse, I grab my badge and federal ID and set them on the counter. As I do, the photograph catches my eye. I barely recognize the picture of myself. The woman shown has a sharp gaze, a confident air about her. So different from the mess I feel like now.

I'm determined to get that version of me back. Until I do, I'll just have to keep faking it. Mustering an authority I don't feel, I say, "If you call now, you should receive authorization by the time I've finished shopping."

His spine straightens, head drawing back as he takes another look at me, reassessing the situation with this new information. "Hey, Stew?"

A twentysomething looks up from where he's chatting with a couple of guys who appear to be just hanging out and asks, "Yeah?"

"Do me a favor and get the NICS approval for this purchase for me while I finish helping her."

The kid comes over, eyebrows almost meeting his hairline as he spots my identification. He looks from me to the badge several times, an eager grin spreading across his face. "I can finish helping her."

"Just make the call, Stew."

"Yeah." He rubs at the patchy scrub growing across his cheeks with poorly disguised disappointment. "Sure thing."

"Now then," the man returns his attention to me. "Did you want red dots for any of them?"

It's a valid question. While a great many of my coworkers—and shooters in general—use red dots to help improve their time and accuracy, I have an astigmatism that makes them blurry, defeating their purpose, so I shoot iron sights. But what if Jake had to use one of the guns? It might be helpful.

"I'll take that SIG P226, too. Let's add one to that."

"You still want a .45?"

"Yes."

He gestures for me to follow, leading the way to a display at the back of the store. "You want to stick with SIG?"

"Actually, I'll take the Glock."

"You need ammo?"

"I'll take a hundred rounds for each of the pistols. Frangible, if you have it."

"I do."

"Perfect. I'll also take a box of twenty-five slugs for the shotgun."

He nods, grabbing boxes from a shelf on the wall behind him and stacking them on the counter before me. "Anything else?"

"An extra clip for each. And holsters. An IWB for the P229, paddle for the others."

Usually, I'd wear an ankle holster for the piece I intend to conceal, but it's too hot right now to wear pants. Until my blood thins from being back in the heat, an "inside the waistband" will have to do.

"That should be it," I say.

He leads me over to the register and looks at Stew, who gives him a thumbs up. I take a deep breath and brace myself for the total, handing my credit card over. Sign the receipt and gather my bags from the counter.

"Ma'am." His voice is so low that I barely hear him. It's his hand on my arm that makes me stop. I give him a questioning look. "I understand that you might not be able to tell me, but my kids go to school around here. Is there something getting ready to go down that I should worry about?"

I understand why he would think that. I just came in here and armed myself like I'm preparing to go into battle. But what can I tell him to make him feel better about the safety of his family? That I just came from a shrink appointment where I was forced to talk about a traumatic experience? That I'm just being paranoid?

I'm not sure that I am. And as for his kids, it's a dangerous world that we live in. He should be on guard as far as they're concerned. But I suspect saying so wouldn't be telling him anything he doesn't already know.

Patting his hand, I give him my first genuine smile since I entered the store. "If there's anything specific that you need to be worried about, it's nothing I'm aware of. I just came down here without packing properly. Turns out I'm not made for traveling light."

I give a small laugh as I leave the store, hoping that I've done a decent job of reassuring him. Maybe at least someone will sleep well tonight. It's just too bad it won't be me.

CHAPTER 13

Driving back to Gator Glade, I feel angry, ashamed, and confused. Surely one gun would have been enough. Instead, I bought half the store. Did I just make another rash decision?

No. Not if it means keeping Jake and myself safe. Not if it makes me feel better. But has it? Also no. I still feel scared and vulnerable.

But it's not only my fault that I feel this way. If Sheriff Kingston was taking things more seriously, maybe I wouldn't be so worried right now, but he's not, which means I can't rely on local law enforcement for backup.

I can't help wondering if Sheriff Kingston would be acting differently if I were someone else. Someone besides the swamp scum who had the nerve to date his son back in high school. Who then went on to enrage them both when she found a way to escape the toxic situation.

It would be sad if that's true. It's sad even if it's not.

He took an oath to protect the people of Gator Glade. As far as I can tell, he's failing, and that pisses me off. I latch on to the anger, fanning the coals until they ignite. I can't allow my fear to paralyze me. And I can't just sit around and wait for answers, hoping they fall into my lap.

Taking the turn into Gator Glade, I head straight for the small building that houses the sheriff's department. But as I drive past the fenced-in dirt patch beside it that's used as an impound lot, I see that it's empty.

Cursing, I pull a U-turn in the middle of the street and backtrack to the edge of town, bumping my way down the narrow dirt road that leads to the scrapyard. As I pass through the dilapidated gate, a memory hits me hard enough to knock me breathless.

When I was a kid, there was a rumor that the cantankerous old man who owned the place, Jethro Keene, had a pet bobcat that guarded the lot at night instead of a dog. Even though we doubted it was true, no one had the nerve to climb the fence after hours to find out for sure, no matter how many times they were dared.

Dogs will do their job, but cats? They'll torture and toy with their prey for amusement. It was an effective threat.

I figured if anyone would know for sure if it was true or not, it would be Butch, but any time I asked my grandfather, he'd just smile mysteriously and shrug. Tell me that unless I had a valid reason to visit the place after daylight, there was no need to find out. I never did.

I never visited period until now. And though I figured Old Man Keene would have long since retired, as I walk inside the small trailer used as an office, I discover that I was mistaken. I press my lips together, trying to conceal my surprise.

The man is now ancient. He squints at me, then says, "Cassidy Knox."

"Yes, sir." I'm shocked he knows my name. Even more so that he recognizes me since I've been away a couple of decades.

"Meant to catch up with you at Butch's funeral to pay my respects. Never got the chance."

"I'm sorry about that," I say, trying to think of a reason other than the truth for why I ran off so quickly from the viewing a little over a week ago.

But it turns out it isn't necessary.

His expression softens as he says, "My daughter works for the state police. She told me what you discovered that day. It must have been a shock to find out that your grandfather had been murdered. Even worse to be the one to figure it out."

I nod, speechless.

"She also told me that you killed the lowlife scum who did it. I'm glad. Butch was a good man. He deserved better."

Another nod as I wonder if I should be concerned that when I think of the trauma I've experienced recently, the things I'm supposed to be talking about in therapy, that putting two bullets into the head of the person who murdered my grandfather isn't among them.

Considering it's the reason my leave was extended, and I was ordered back into therapy after Director Jacobson had intervened to get me out of it, it feels like it should hold more significance. But whether it's because it was the second life I had taken in under a month, or that I feel vindicated for having taken it, it's not something I'm at risk of losing sleep over.

Too bad there are plenty of other things to keep me awake at night.

"What brings you here?" he asks.

I shake my head, clearing my thoughts.

"There was a car crash out by the sanctuary yesterday. I didn't see the truck in the impound lot. I was wondering if it was brought here instead."

"What if it was?"

"Can I see it?"

"Why?"

"Because I'm fairly certain there was a second vehicle involved."

"Shouldn't be here if that's the truth."

Holding his gaze, I say, "Exactly."

Jethro pulls a stack of papers closer to him and flips through it. Removes one and groans as he gets up, his stooped figure far less imposing than the one I remember from my youth. "I'll go with you. Want to take a look for myself."

Though his steps shuffle, they're quicker than I expect as he leads the way out a back door to the scrapyard beyond. I scan the hunks of rusted metal we pass as we walk, some twisted and misshapen, others scalped down to the mere bones of their frames. Finally, we come to a stop in front of the truck I'd found wrapped around a tree just yesterday.

"Well, will you look at that," he says, shading his eyes against the glare of the sun.

"Did you take the plate off?" I ask.

He scans the paper in his hand. "Didn't come in with one."

Odd. The license plate had been on it when I saw the vehicle. And Sheriff Kingston told me the tag had been reported as stolen. He must have kept it. I file the information away and squat down beside the damaged right rear panel.

"There's paint transfer," I say, mostly to myself.

"Wonder why the sheriff didn't hold on to this a bit longer 'til he could figure out if it was from yesterday's wreck or not."

"Probably because I suggested he do just that."

The old man snorts behind me. "You just might be right. Whatcha doing there?"

Using one of my keys, I scrape some of the out-of-place paint into a small plastic vial. One that I keep in my purse for reasons like this. "Just taking a sample. Is that all right?"

"I suppose it'll have to be. It's already done." He gives me a sharp look. "You think that paint is from the vehicle that caused the crash?"

"I do."

Standing, I circle the truck. Reaching the driver's side, I peer at the dash, confirming what the sheriff had told me about the Vehicle Identification Number having been removed.

"If you're looking for the VIN, there isn't one."

He taps the paper as if to prove his statement as I turn to face him. "Do you get a lot of vehicles in here without VINs?"

"Considering it's illegal to remove them? No. Says here that my boy pointed it out to Sheriff Kingston, but he told him not to worry about it."

"Huh."

"You don't sound impressed with his detective work," he remarks.

"That's because I'm not."

"You want me to tow this to the back, keep it out of sight in one of my bays until you figure this out?"

"Would you?"

"I'll go get the tow truck and do it now."

"Thank you," I say, falling into step beside him as we head back to the office.

He nods. "You're moving back here now, aren't you? Gonna take over running the sanctuary?"

"I am."

"Good. It's been too long since we've had someone to do a decent job of enforcing the law around here."

"Oh, I'm not looking to be an officer."

He smirks. "I never said you were."

Getting back in my car, I watch through the fence as

he climbs into his tow truck and pulls around back, thinking about what he said. I've already decided to stay in Gator Glade. And to retire from law enforcement.

But will I really be able to look the other way when I see something wrong happening? If the paint samples I just took are any example, it's not likely. Which means I have two choices. I can either follow the rules—or make my own.

CHAPTER 14

My heart punches against the walls of my chest. I'm strung tighter than a piano, muscles bunched into knots beneath my skin. My teeth grind together painfully, fingers clenched around the steering wheel.

Any way you look at it, a crime has been committed. Whether a second vehicle was involved in the wreck or not, removing a VIN is a felony. The truck the woman was driving is evidence. Sheriff Kingston knows that. And the fact that he sent it to the scrapyard anyway? To say that I'm angry would be an understatement.

And what am I supposed to do with the paint samples I collected? Send them to a private lab? Call in a favor with coworkers at the FBI? Then what? The results are useless without access to the databases I need to trace them to the culprit. I growl in frustration.

As much as I long to drive to the sheriff's department and confront Kingston, I know that isn't the answer. Though it might make me feel better to tell the man what I think about him and his shoddy police work, I can't.

There are too many unknowns. Too much is as stake.

If he finds out I'm conducting my own investigation, he'll do his best to make things more difficult for me which means I need to have patience, at least until I get a chance to talk to the woman who crashed and find out her version of what really happened. But patience isn't exactly one of my strong suits.

Which is why I make the call before I have a chance to second-guess my decision. And though a part of me almost wishes she won't answer, all of me is relieved when she does.

"Cassidy! I was just thinking about you. How's it going down there?"

Closing my eyes, I lean my head back against the seat and conjure an image of Mallory Chan's eternally cheerful face.

"It's going good."

"When will you be back?"

The question catches me off guard. I guess I just assumed that my coworkers hadn't expected me to return. Not given the mess I'd become before I left. But Mallory's not the type to pretend out of politeness.

After a long pause, I answer, "I don't think I am."

"What? Why not? You're Jacobson's favorite. There's no way she'd let them get rid of you. And you and I both know this is what you were born to do. So what gives?"

"It's complicated."

"What's his name?"

I stutter as I try to think of a reply, making her laugh.

"Girl, you are so busted. Now come on. I need details. Consider it the price of the favor you're going to ask."

I feel horrible that I'm the kind of friend who will only call when I need something, but Mallory knows me. Until I came down here, I ate, slept, and breathed the job. I'd rather solve a crime than be social.

That mutual understanding formed the basis of our friendship. She knows she can always count on me in the way I'm counting on her now. So I concede.

"Jake Walker."

"Jake Walker," she repeats, drawing out the name in a way that lets me know she's typing it into one of the criminal databases at her disposal.

"Oh my."

I bite my lip to keep from smiling, but it doesn't work.

"*Oh* my," she repeats. "Is there more than one Jake Walker in Gator Glade?"

"No."

"I'm not sure I've ever seen someone who was actually charged with jaywalking before."

"Yeah, the local sheriff had it out for him when we were younger."

"Looks like he's behaved himself for the last twenty years. Does he still look anything like his old booking photo?"

"Better."

"Okay, I officially hate you. Unless he has a brother?"

"Sorry."

Mallory sighs heavily into the phone. "It's okay. And for the record, I totally get why you'd want to stay down there, but are you sure?"

"I am."

"And he treats you well?"

"Yes."

"He listens to you?"

"I told him he was mine when I was four and he still believes me, so yeah."

"You know I'm going to spend all my vacations visiting you now, right?"

"I'd be disappointed if you didn't."

"Good. Now that that's settled, what can I help you with?"

I fill her in on what's happened—the wreck, the silent Jane Doe, my suspicions that a second vehicle was involved, and the sheriff sending the truck to the scrapyard despite the removed VIN number, ending with the transferred paint flakes I removed from the dent.

"Send them to me. I'll see if the lab can narrow down the make and model of the second vehicle," she says. "And text me everything you have on Jane Doe's truck. I'll see if I can find any matches that were reported stolen."

"That would be great, thanks.

"Can I share this with Director Jacobson? I'm asking because I can't put in a request for magneto-optical imaging, but it's possible that she could."

"Magneto what?"

"Basically, it's when they use a magnetic field to help visualize anomalies in the base metal. Our lab uses it a lot on firearms that have had the serial numbers removed, but it can help recover VINs too. I'm sure the Miami field office must have one."

I debate for only a moment. As reluctant as I am to prolong my dependence on Director Jacobson, if it can get me the answers I need about Jane Doe—and in turn, possibly the people who broke into my house—I can't say no. I'll take all the help I can get on this.

"Yeah, sure."

"Awesome. I'll let her know then get started on seeing if I can't trace the description of the truck to ones reported missing while I'm waiting on the sample."

"Mallory?"

"Yeah?"

"Thank you. For everything."

"Of course, girl. What are friends for?"

"When you come down to visit, the drinks will be on me."

"And if your man has any cute friends…"

"I'll have them lined up and waiting."

"You know me so well. I can't imagine what I'm going to do without you."

"Probably get your job done."

"Ha. Where's the fun in that?" Though she laughs, she sounds sad as she says, "You be careful, Cassidy, do you hear me? If anything happens to you and I lose my vacation home in Florida, I'm gonna be devastated."

Though I'd felt myself relax during the conversation with my friend, as I end the call and start the drive to the post office to overnight the paint samples, I feel my muscles bunching back into knots. Because Mallory knows me. Not many people do, but she does.

There's no reason, based on what I told her, for her to be worried about my safety. But she is. Which means she heard what I left unsaid. And she believed it.

CHAPTER 15

I'm not one of those people who can be trusted alone with their thoughts. This was true even before I woke up in a serial killer's basement. Or discovered my grandfather had been murdered. The truth is, they've always been too dark. And the darkness has always made me feel a bit desperate.

It's possible that's why I joined the FBI—so I'd always have a noble purpose to keep me busy. Only, that isn't the case anymore. I don't have access to an endless parade of evil. Just that which directly affects me.

Perhaps that's why the stakes feel so high. So dangerous.

And it's entirely possible I'm blowing things out of proportion to create a distraction for myself. But even realizing that, when I called the hospital again and found out I still couldn't visit Jane Doe, I felt a surge of panic spreading beneath my skin.

I couldn't just do nothing, not when there were so many questions that still needed answers. Yet there was no denying that in terms of investigating, I'd hit a wall. Every avenue I could think of relied on someone else for the next step. And I've never been good at waiting. So I knew I had to find a way to stay occupied.

Which is how I find myself here, in Butch's room, covering the once-white walls, yellowed by age, with a fresh coat of pale-blue paint. And though each stroke feels like a tiny blow to my soul, there's something therapeutic about it as well.

It's not like I'm trying to erase Butch. There's no chance of that. My memories of my grandfather are firmly ingrained into every cell of my body—he's part of who I am.

But it needs to be done. Every time I look at the missing rectangle of carpet in the living room, I'm reminded of why it was removed, the blood that stained it. Some of it Jake's.

The flooring needs to be replaced. It only makes sense to paint first. And to start in Butch's room, since it's already empty.

Besides… it isn't Butch's room anymore. Coming to terms with that is part of moving on. Part of the healing process. It's healthy.

But then why does it feel like such a betrayal?

"Wow."

I jump, the paint roller dropping from my hand onto the carpet.

"Sorry." Jake gives me an apologetic smile as I turn to face him. "I didn't mean to startle you. Let me help you clean up the mess."

I do a double take as I take him in. His white button-down shirt rolled up at the sleeves, tucked into a pair of gray slacks, a tie hanging loosely around his neck. I'm not used to seeing him dressed like this.

But I'm not complaining. I tear my gaze away and glance behind me to survey the damage, then shrug.

"No, it's fine."

"You sure?"

"I'll be pulling up the carpet soon anyway," I say, joining him by the doorway.

"Yeah, I saw the flooring boxes in the living room.

You know how to put that stuff down?"

"Sure." I don't, but I figure it can't be too hard. The boxes say easy DIY installation right on them. Besides, figuring it out will keep me busy longer.

"I like the color."

"Yeah?" I turn to survey my work.

"Yeah." Looping his good arm around my waist, he pulls me to him, kissing my neck. "I especially love how it looks here." Another kiss. "And here." A little lower. "And here."

I shiver as his lips touch the spot where my neck meets my shoulder. A jolt of electricity spreads through me, leaving my nerve endings tingling. I want to lose myself in this. In him. But we aren't supposed to do that right now, no matter how much I want to.

"I'm a mess, aren't I?"

"Not at all."

I turn my head and give him a look. He grins.

"Maybe a little. But it suits you."

I stifle a sigh. If he only knew how wrong he is, the way it's done my head in to have my thoughts and emotions in such disarray.

"Are you okay?" he asks.

"Yeah. Why?"

"I don't know." He tightens his arm around me. "You just seem a little sad, I guess."

I lean against him, glad he can't see my expression. "It's just…" my voice breaks as I gesture toward Butch's room.

"Aw, Cassie." He spins me around, pulling me to his chest. I nestle against him, eyes squeezed shut as I do my best not to cry. "You know this is what he'd want. For you to make this place your own. To not… dwell on the past."

We both know that's just Jake's polite way of saying

to move on and not get caught up in mourning. But he's right.

Though it was a tough lesson to learn, it's one I was taught repeatedly as a child. I was only five when I lost my parents, but even then, Butch did his best to get me to focus on celebrating their lives instead of brooding over their deaths.

And with the steady stream of animals that came to the sanctuary over the years, loss was a constant I came to know well. But he never let me spend too much time with my grief. Drawing a deep breath, I nod.

"You're right."

"Those are very sexy words to hear a woman say."

I pull away so he can see the glare I'm aiming at him, but that lopsided smile he's giving me makes it tough to maintain.

"Let me take you out tonight. A date."

"No, you must be tired."

"I insist."

"I'm a mess."

"So take a shower."

"But I still have to feed—"

"I'll handle it."

"You're supposed to be taking it easy," I remind him.

"And I will. Promise. See? I'm wearing the sling. I have been all day. If you think I'm going to do anything to risk dragging this injury out even a second longer…"

The look he's giving me makes me blush. And the idea of being here alone with him all night with nothing to occupy our time but think about what we'd both rather be doing? The heat creeping up my neck is starting to make me sweat.

"Okay," I agree. "I'll be quick."

His voice is low as he says, "I won't be." The look

he gives me as he backs out of the room makes me swallow hard. "But I'll have everyone fed and watered in a jiffy."

I hold onto the doorframe as I watch him leave, realizing that there's more than one kind of trouble to be in. And while some of those kinds might be more fun than others, I'm not sure they're any less dangerous. Because life hurts more when you have something you want to hold on to.

CHAPTER 16

The restaurant is fancier than I expected. Real tablecloths, wine by the bottle, entrees that cost as much as a tank of gas kind of fancy. And as Jake gives his name to the maître d' and we're shown to a table against a window overlooking the water, I realize that he had this all planned in advance.

Candles cast the room in a warm glow just bright enough to read the menu, but the low lighting doesn't make me feel any less self-conscious. I wanted to wear a dress, but the only one I packed when I came down was the one for Butch's funeral. So I'd raided my old closet, pulling out a little cocktail number from one of my high school homecoming dances.

Though the fabric is in surprisingly good condition for something over twenty years old, the cut is a little snugger than I remember. More likely it's my body that's changed, but either way, the end result is the same, the material pulling tight over curves I didn't used to have.

But the way Jake keeps looking at those curves? It makes me feel confident and sexy, proud of my body.

My guard lowers in a way I'm not used to. It takes me out of my head, where everything's dark and tragic and frightening. Everything that's been bothering me slips away as I lose myself in the moment, enjoying the food, the wine, the company. The way his knees rub against mine beneath the table. The moon glinting off the water beyond the window.

Until now, I didn't believe in perfect, but this night feels straight out of a fairytale. And as we're walking back to the car after dinner, I find myself disappointed that it's coming to an end. Jake unlocks the door but doesn't open it. He turns to me with a hopeful look.

"You want to go for a walk along the water?" he asks.

I don't hesitate an instant before saying, "Yes."

He helps steady me as I slip my shoes off, then removes his own. We toss them in the car, laughing as we limp across the parking lot until we reach the sand.

Taking my hand in his, our fingers lace together as we make our way down to the shoreline, and I'm transported back in time to when we were kids, before our lives took the complicated twists that kept us apart.

He really is just the grown version of the little boy who captured my heart. The one I planned a future with before I even knew what that really entailed.

No one else has ever made me feel like he does. Even as a child, I somehow knew. I feel a pang of regret for all the years I stayed away, wondering what our lives would look like now if I'd come back sooner.

But I'm here now. That's what matters. That, and making sure that being with me isn't a threat to Jake's safety.

I glance over to find him watching me with a curious expression on his face.

"What?" I ask.

"I was just wondering. Have you given any thought to when you're going to go up to Virginia to pack up your apartment?"

"No. Why?"

Reaching a series of pilings embedded in the beach,

we turn around and head back to the car.

"I was just thinking that maybe I'd go with you," he says cautiously, studying my reaction.

"Really?" I'm unable to contain my smile. It falls a moment later. "What about the animals?"

"I know someone who can watch them while we're gone."

"What about work?"

"Where do you think I'd rather be? There or with you?"

My smile returns. I squeeze his hand a little tighter.

"I was thinking we could fly up. Rent a U-Haul to drive back down."

"That would be great."

"Yeah?"

We come to a stop at the edge of the parking lot, turning to face each other. The streetlights give me a clearer look at his face, and I notice a hint of tension at his brow. It makes me wonder if he's concerned about me going alone because he's worried that I won't come back.

But he doesn't need to be concerned about that. By his side is the only place I want to be.

Reaching up, I run my hand along his face. Touch my thumb to his lower lip as I cup his jaw in my palm, lowering his head toward mine.

"I know it's been almost thirty-five years since the last time I told you this, but you're mine and I'm yours, Jake Walker. And now I'm old enough to fight anyone who tries to take you away. You're stuck with me. You might as well get used to it."

I pray it's true as our lips meet. I savor the feel of it, of his body as it presses against mine, his slinged arm pinned between us, his hand so close to my breast that I ache for its touch.

Someone clears their throat obnoxiously loud, but I refuse to end this moment. I rise up on my toes as Jake lifts his head, maintaining contact.

"You know, you used to have class."

My body goes rigid, recognizing the voice. I still hear it in my dreams sometimes, though never the good ones.

"But I guess that disappeared along with your standards."

"Let's go," I whisper to Jake, refusing to look at Matt Kingston.

Just breathing the same air as my old high school boyfriend makes me tense. And remembering the way he used his dad's power as the town's sheriff to keep me trapped in a relationship with him until I was able to escape by leaving for college makes me angry. The kind of angry that could easily inspire me to do something stupid.

Jake nods, the headlights on the car flashing as he unlocks it.

"I remember that dress, you know."

I keep my gaze aimed at the vehicle, refusing to give Matt the time of day, ignoring him like he doesn't exist.

"More specifically, I remember taking that dress off you."

Jake's hand flinches on my back. I come to a halt. Take a deep breath before responding, because I have to say something. I don't want Jake to think it's true because it's not. If it were, I never would have worn it on our first official date.

"That's bull and you know it," I say, working to keep my voice calm. "I wore this dress to homecoming senior year. The same year you passed out drunk, covered in your own vomit in the bed of Jeff Scott's truck before we even made it inside."

I turn to look at him and find my old best friend, Tracey Vale, hanging off his arm, trying to pull him away. I would have liked to rekindle my friendship with Tracey. Unfortunately, Matt's lingering interest in me has prevented that.

"Since you probably don't remember, ask Tracey. She was there. She can tell you how relieved I was to be rid of you. You never even touched this dress." Making eye contact with Jake, I add, "And *that's* the truth."

Taking him by the hand, I tug him toward the car, Matt calling me obscenities as we walk away. But it doesn't matter. *He* doesn't matter. The only thing that does is right here beside me, and I'm not going to let some mistake from the past ruin what's been a wonderful night.

Reality can take a raincheck. I have other plans.

CHAPTER 17

I've changed my mind. I don't want to be here anymore. It's strange, because as much as I'd been obsessing over this only yesterday, a part of me dreads what I'm about to do. Because after my date with Jake last night, I no longer want to peer into the dark shadows that surround me, looking for trouble.

I just want to be happy. And if what that takes is burying my head in the sand and pretending danger doesn't exist, I'm inclined to do it.

Only, every time I think about walking away, I see the woman's face.

I don't even know her name. But I know her fear.

What I saw in her eyes the day of the wreck was unmistakable. She was running from something. Even if her accident has nothing to do with the break-in at my place, she needs my help. I can't just walk away from that, no matter how much I'd like to.

So I arrive at the hospital early, just in time for visiting hours, trying to convince myself that I'm still eager to get some answers. Wind my way around the parking garage, searching for a spot. Ignore the unsettled feeling in my stomach telling me that this is a bad idea.

As I get out of my car, a list of all the things I should do today fills my mind. I need to put a second coat of paint on the walls in Butch's old bedroom. Then I ought to cut the carpet into strips so it will be easier to move after I pull it up. Once it's gone, I can paint the baseboards.

I'm so lost in thought that by the time I notice the second set of steps echoing across the parking garage, I have no idea how long someone's been walking behind me. It isn't normal for me to be so unaware of my surroundings. Considering everything that's been going on, it isn't smart either.

A ripple of unease spreads under my skin, causing me to quicken my gait. The person behind me quickens theirs as well. And they're close. Too close.

I brush my hand over my hip, feeling for a gun that isn't there. That's right. I hadn't wanted to risk getting hung up by hospital security, so I left it at home.

Feeling like an idiot, I slip my hand into my purse. Grabbing my phone, I brush my thumb over the sensor, unlocking the screen. I bring up the camera app and switch it to selfie mode, raising the device with both hands so I can zoom in from over my shoulder and get a look at whoever's approaching behind me.

All the screen shows is a flash of movement. Then everything is dark. The chemical stench of burlap fills my nose as the rough material is drawn tight, my hands pulled hard against my face by the hood, my phone knocking painfully into my nose.

Instinctively, I jerk forward at the waist. My assailant holds on, their weight heavy on my back as their feet leave the ground. Then I straighten with a snap, simultaneously punching out against the sack with both fists. Their face smashes against the back of my skull.

The move leaves me dizzy, but it's worth it—it loosens their hold enough for me to slip the hood off over my head. Keeping a handful of the material clenched in one fist, I spin to face them, trying to loop the now empty burlap sack around their wrists.

But I only manage to snare one of them before my attacker drops a shoulder and charges, slamming my spine against the side of a van, my head hitting the metal so hard I see stars. They wrap a hand around my throat, keeping me pinned to the vehicle.

I raise a knee, confirming my attacker is male. He grunts, doubling over. I drive an elbow into the back of his neck, then send him stumbling backward as I shove his shoulders.

He's several feet away when he catches his balance. And I've got my fists up, ready to fight.

My chest heaves, nostrils flaring as we face off. Behind the mask he wears—the same creepy white mask worn by the duo who broke into my house—his eyes are a startling shade of blue. And any confidence that was once in them is gone.

He lifts an arm, pointing a finger at me. It wavers in the air between us. Then he turns and runs.

The act takes me by surprise. By the time I take off after him, he's rounding the corner. Tires squeal. Brakes screech. When I reach the end of the row, he's gone.

I pant heavily as I retrace my steps back to the site of the attack and grab the burlap sack off the cement. My body trembles as I stare at the makeshift hood.

What did he plan to do once he had it secured over my head? Abduct me? Or worse?

Though the thought of what almost happened makes me feel ill, there's another that makes me even sicker. Whoever it was, whatever his reason, he's still out there.

CHAPTER 18

I'm sitting in front of a bank of monitors inside the security room at the hospital when there's a knock on the door. I flinch, adrenaline still coursing through my veins like floodwaters through a broken dam. And the gate that keeps the fight or flight hormone in check inside me just might be in permanent disrepair.

It's hard to imagine ever feeling relaxed again. My muscles are strung tight, my nerves even tighter. The idea of letting my guard down seems like a bad one. But when the door opens and a nurse sticks her head through the gap, holding an ice pack out to me with a sympathetic look, I feel foolish.

"You sure you don't want me to get a doctor to check you?"

I attempt a smile, but it falls flat. "I'm sure. Thanks."

The head of hospital security opens his mouth like he's about to object but decides otherwise. He watches me like I make him anxious. Like I might panic and decide to strike out at anyone around me.

I wait until the nurse leaves the room, then debate where on my body to ice. My nose feels stuffy and swollen. Somehow, I ended up with a fat lip. And my entire body feels like I've been used as a human pinata.

But as the security guard settles back in his seat, the footage from the parking garage appearing on a screen before us, and I notice the dent in the side of the van I hit, right about skull height, I decide on the back of my head.

Lines mar the black-and-white video as it goes in reverse. I close my eyes as the image shows the man running backward from around the corner.

"Do you have any cameras that show where he went? What type of car he was driving?" I ask.

"Unfortunately, no. We only have units inside the garage. Once he turned that corner, he was outside our coverage area."

Great. So now, on top of being afraid to relax at home or when out in public, I'll have to be looking over my shoulder whenever I drive, worried about being followed, too. And I won't even know what kind of vehicle to watch out for.

"You ready?" he asks.

I open my eyes to find him looking at me with concern.

"Yeah. Can you give me a copy of the footage as well?"

He pulls a face. "I'm really not supposed to."

I match his expression. "I realize that this is more a local police matter than FBI, but I'd really hate to get them involved. Somehow, these type of incidents always get leaked to the media."

The way he eyes me lets me know he's not sure if I'm trying to be helpful, or if I'm making a threat. The truth is, I'm not quite sure myself. I suppose it depends on whether I get my way or not.

"You got an email I can send it to?"

I nod, taking the pen and paper he offers me and writing it down. As I do, I ask, "And you'll put a guard on the woman's room? The Jane Doe?"

"Trust me. After what happened to you today, no one

is getting on her floor—or any other—without proper identification. But yes, we'll keep a special eye out on her room since you suspect she might be somehow involved."

"Thank you."

"Okay. Here we go."

My stomach roils as I watch myself walking across the parking garage, completely lost in my own little world. As the man in the mask, who I can now see is wearing the same black hoodie and flashy shoes that he wore when he broke into my house, stalks up behind me. As he pulls the burlap sack over my head.

The struggle between us takes a fraction of the time as it seemed to when we were engaged in battle. I can feel the guard's eyes yoyoing between me and the screen. When the ordeal is over, my assailant running around the corner, disappearing from view, he releases a low whistle.

"You really gave him what for, didn't you?"

I shrug, the lump in my throat too big to reply.

"They teach you those moves at the Bureau?"

"No." It comes out as a whisper. Though we'd been taught basic self-defense moves at the academy, that's not where I learned to fight. I have Butch to thank for that. Butch who, for some reason, insisted that I practice sparring with him as soon as I was old enough to throw an effective punch.

He's also the one who trained me in how to shoot. Wilderness survival. Extensive first aid. And who ingrained in me so much more practical knowledge that I didn't properly appreciate at the time. I owe my life to his training several times over now.

It's almost like he knew that I'd need the skills someday.

"Well, you should get the video any minute now. I

just sent it."

My phone dings, the notification flashing on the screen. I clear my throat, standing. "Thank you."

"You want me to walk you out?"

"That's okay. I want to check on the Jane Doe before I leave."

"I'll have Patsy help you." Following me to the door, he sticks his head out into the hall. "Hey, Patsy? Can you show her to the Jane Doe who was in that car accident?"

The nurse who brought me the ice pack earlier hurries over. "Sure thing. Follow me, hun."

I ignore the curious glances she gives me as we walk down the hall. As we wait for an elevator, then take it up to the third floor. As our steps bounce off the walls of a second hallway.

Finally, she stops in front of a closed door and opens it. I look inside to see the nameless woman from the crash lying in the hospital bed, sleeping.

"Do you mind if I wake her?" I ask.

Nurse Patsy squints at a whiteboard hanging on the wall across from the bed. "I don't think you could if you tried. They had to sedate her earlier. She was agitated, kept trying to remove her IV."

"Do you have any idea what had her so upset?"

"No clue. She still hasn't said anything yet."

"Nothing?"

"Not one word."

Why would the woman maintain her silence? Why hasn't she asked for help?

The adrenaline that had finally eased in my system ramps back up as I cross the room. Once again, I'm struck by a strange sense of recognition as I look at her. Only, now that the blood has been cleaned off of her, I notice other things as well.

"Do you have any idea what happened to her arm?"

I ask, pointing to a series of cuts much too uniform in size and spacing to have been caused by the wreck.

"No. It's not an injury I've seen caused by a car accident before."

I take in the woman's split lip, the cut bisecting her eyebrow, her blackened eye. But it's the bruising to her left hand that I find most curious, her fingertips swollen and discolored, blood extending up the beds of her nails. Almost like she'd had something shoved beneath them. Like she'd been tortured.

I rub at my chest, trying to ease the gathering tension, though I know it's useless. Not when I've gained no answers, only more questions. Because the only thing I know for sure is that this isn't over yet.

CHAPTER 19

It's obvious someone's after me. That became clear the instant I recognized the plain white mask my attacker in the parking lot wore as the same type used by the people who broke into my house. But things just got much more complicated.

It's funny how money can do that. Not mine though. Theirs.

Knowing that these people are well funded makes the situation feel more dangerous. And they definitely have cash to squander.

These aren't junkies trying to scrounge up enough cash for their next fix. Which means I have something else that they want—and I have no clue what that is.

I'd wanted answers. It was my desperation to gather any kind of information to work with that compelled me to sit here at the kitchen table, comparing the video from the break-in side-by-side to the footage of the attack in the hospital parking garage. To search frame by frame, no matter how unsettled it made me feel.

But the masks are generic. The black hoodies could have been bought anywhere. For all I know, the burlap sack had been weathering in someone's shed for years. The only unique features were the ones on the man's feet.

Ten years ago, I would have spent hours if not days poring over pictures in a database looking for a match for the shoes that my assailant wore, and I still might not have come up with a hit. Today, it took me less than a minute to screenshot the image and get a link to the exact footwear using Google Lens.

Sixty seconds to feel the world beneath me shift. Because the shoes he wore weren't just flashy. They're expensive. Two thousand three hundred and ninety-five dollars before tax, according to the Neiman Marcus website where the Christian Louboutin sneakers are listed for sale.

I'm still staring at the screen when I hear the front door open. A moment later, Jake sets his briefcase down on the chair across from me. I look at his feet.

"How much did your shoes cost?" I ask.

"My shoes?" he looks down at them. "I don't know. Why?"

"Ballpark range," I press. "One hundred? One thousand?"

His eyes widen and he gives me a funny look when I say the word thousand.

"Less than two hundred."

So, a partner at one of the ritziest, most prestigious corporate law firms in the state spends less   than   ten percent on the Oxfords he wears to work than what a criminal spent on the sneakers he wore to attack me.

"What's going on?" Jake asks, settling into the seat beside me. Then, as he catches a glimpse of my face, no longer concealed by the computer screen, "Cassie, what happened?"

I gingerly touch my lip, knowing that's what looks the worst. I wish I could lie but know that I can't.

"I was attacked in the parking garage at the hospital this morning."

"This morning? Why didn't you call me?"

"I didn't want to bother you," I lie, unable to let

myself confess the truth—that after the adrenaline wore off, all I could think about was Jake. The desire to hear his voice, see his face, to feel his arms around me overridden only by my need to keep him safe and away from this, whatever it is.

"That's not something that falls under the term "bother" and you know it. Did they at least catch the guy?"

"No."

Jake curses, slipping out of the chair to squat beside me. He cups my cheek gently in his hand, turning my head to face him.

"Was he trying to steal your purse or something?"

I shake my head. His gaze drifts from me to the computer screen. To the two open windows with surveillance videos. A third at the bottom with the page to the shoes.

He swallows loudly. The images are paused on the frame that shows the clearest shot of the man's footwear. In the case of the parking garage footage, it's when the man has just pulled the hood over my head.

Jake's voice cracks as he asks, "Is that you?"

"Yes."

"I think you should go back to Virginia for a while."

"That's not happening."

"Not forever. Just until they catch this guy."

"Who's *they*, Jake?"

"The police."

The look I give him makes him curse again. He takes both my hands in his, his eyes begging me. "Will you at least forget about the woman in the wreck and focus on your own safety?"

"I can't."

"You could if you wanted to."

"That's not true. Jake, that guy broke into this house

before the woman crashed into the tree. Whatever's going on here is related. Our safety might depend on her safety." Giving his hands a squeeze, I say, "I understand that this is scary, but she knows something. I have to find out what."

He pulls away and stands, pinching the bridge of his nose as he slumps against the counter. "I'm not trying to boss you around, Cassie. I'm just worried."

Slipping out of my seat, I move to join him. "I know."

"I just got you back. I can't lose you."

"You won't."

"How can you be so sure? Some guy just tried to abduct you from a public parking lot."

"And he learned a very important lesson about messing with me."

"Yeah. That he needs to try harder to incapacitate you before getting close enough for you to hurt him. Which means next time he'll probably bring some friends to help."

"So will I." I gesture to the counter behind him, where my purchases from the gun store yesterday are laid out. Grabbing the pistol with the red dot I bought for him, I ask, "Can you shoot?"

"Yes." He takes the firearm from me with a sigh and sets it down. "But I don't want to. Let's go away. If you don't want to pack up your apartment, we'll go somewhere else. Anywhere you want. Name a place and I'll make it happen."

"That won't solve anything."

"It might."

"And it might make a bigger problem to deal with when we come back. They might take their frustration out on the sanctuary. On the animals. I can't risk that happening."

"I don't know what you expect me to do, Cassie."

"Nothing. Only maybe… maybe you should stay at your place for a while. Just until whatever's going on here blows over."

He looks at me like I just suggested we take up hunting endangered species. His voice is low as he asks, "Do you really think that I'd agree to that? Now? With everything that's happened?"

I didn't, but I had to try. I can't let Jake put himself at risk for me again. And while I doubt that whoever's behind this will try breaking into the house a second time, the instant I suspect otherwise, Jake's gone—no matter what I have to do to make that happen.

My teeth grit together painfully against the tears I'm fighting. Swallowing hard, I say, "I can take care of this."

It feels like I'm trying to convince myself as much as him.

"I think we should hire some security. Just until whatever's going on is over," he says.

"Jake, if these people can afford to drop two grand on a pair of shoes, you think they can't afford to bribe some stranger to look the other way for a few minutes?"

"I don't like this."

I sigh. "Neither do I. And I'm sorry. I know this is my fault. That's why I need to find out what they want. So I can fix this."

"It's not your fault. But…"

"What?"

"I wish you'd let me do something to help instead of shooting down all my ideas."

"I'm just being realistic."

"And I'm just trying to keep you safe."

"I know. And I appreciate that." But the important thing is keeping *him* out of harm's way. I loop my arms around his waist, but he won't look at me. His good hand stays firmly clenched to the edge of the counter beside him, the one in the sling curled in a fist. "I do. But this isn't something that's going to go away on its own."

"I don't understand why you can't call in some favors. Get some help with this."

"I already have."

"You have?"

I nod, swallowing down the lump of guilt that it's not the whole truth. That the help I'm getting has to do with the forensics of trying to learn more about the vehicles involved in the crash. That I haven't told any of my FBI connections about the attack.

How can I expect him to understand that I don't want to be that person? The one who needs others to fight her battles for her. That part of getting my confidence and self-respect back is to take care of my problems on my own.

It doesn't seem very fair to Jake, especially when what's going on affects him as well. But I have to believe that it's the version of myself that I'm trying so hard to get back that he wants to be with, not some weak, shadowy version.

"Any way you look at it, I still need to speak with the Jane Doe and find out what she knows. If she can give me a name, this could have a very simple solution. Even if she can't, I'd like to have a better idea of what I'm dealing with. Does that sound reasonable?"

A muscle in his jaw tics. "You aren't sleeping in the living room tonight, that's for sure."

"Well, neither are you."

"Then what do you suggest?" he asks. Despite his mood, the corners of his lips twitch with the beginnings of a smile.

"I don't know. I'm sure we can figure something out," I say with a grin.

But there's a bad feeling deep in the pit of my stomach. What if my attempt to regain my confidence is clouding my judgment instead?

CHAPTER 20

My mouth is dry. My pulse is racing. Though I tell myself there's nothing to worry about, I'm not quite sure that it's true.

My palms are damp on the steering wheel as the attack from yesterday plays over and over in my mind while I drive, my thoughts playing Devil's advocate. What if I hadn't had my hands up in front of my face, enabling me to get the hood off? What if my attacker had used a weapon? What if a million other possibilities?

Because if even one thing had been changed, what happened could have gone so much differently. Could have ended so much worse.

It's humbling. And sickening. Nausea has kept my stomach empty—I couldn't even force down a cup of coffee before I left the house this morning.

I wish I could take Jake's advice and forget about the mystery woman. Things had still been a bit tense between us when we went to bed last night, squeezed shoulder to shoulder in the tiny single bed, under separate blankets.

As irrational as it might seem, a small part of me resented his concerns, the way they made me feel like he doubted my ability to take care of myself. And I suspect a large part of him resented my refusal to back down and let this be someone else's problem.

But I can't put something so important in another person's hands. Jake doesn't know how far I'm willing to go to make sure he doesn't get hurt again. That's why the only one I truly trust to take care of this properly is the one who will lose most if it's not—me.

When I woke this morning curled against his side, my head nestled on his chest, his arm wrapped tight around me, I knew it was the way I wanted to start every day. I'm pretty sure that's what he wants, too. But in order for us to have that chance, I need to be sure that there's no threat to his safety.

So even though he might feel like I'm taking an unnecessary risk right now, that it isn't my job to figure out what's going on and that I should let the local police handle Jane Doe and what happened to her, there's too much riding on this for me to take a step back.

Because the accident happened in Gator Glade. Chances are Sheriff Kingston isn't making any kind of effort on the woman's behalf. Which means it really is up to me.

As I reach the hospital, I circle all five levels of the parking garage before returning to the ground floor and taking a space as close to the entrance as possible. Even then, I scan my surroundings, making sure I'm alone before exiting my vehicle. I promised Jake I'd be careful, and that's exactly what I intend to do.

I know that I haven't been followed. The circuitous route I took here enabled me to confirm that. But whoever is after me knew I'd be here yesterday. And they must suspect that I'd be back today. This is where I'm at my most vulnerable.

My hands tremble as I walk inside despite being shoved deep in my pockets, one curled around a can of bear spray, the other around a whistle. And yet, despite the precautions, I still hold my breath, listening carefully to every tiny noise around me until I'm inside.

The security guard stationed by the metal detector in the lobby gives me a suspicious look as I hand over the cannister and ask him to hold onto it for me until my return. I see the doubt in his expression, the uncertainty of whether he should even allow me to proceed or not. The fact that he does, despite his obvious misgivings, does not bode well for the false sense of security I've been trying to work up now that I'm here.

I text Jake to let him know that I made it inside safely, then wait in front of the elevators, pretending to study the hospital directory, until I get one to myself. When someone gets on at the second floor, I get off and wait again. I'm taking every precaution, but I can't help wondering if it's even worth the effort.

Because these people know where I live. They know the car I drive. What's to keep them from doing the same thing to me that they did to the woman I'm here to visit—force me off a long, vacant stretch of road? Like the one I'll have to drive to get home.

I give myself a pep talk, assuring myself that I'll walk into the woman's hospital room and she'll tell me everything I need to know. That this will all be over soon.

But the instant I leave the elevator and make eye contact with the nurse from yesterday, Patsy, all the hope I'd been trying to muster disappears. She hops to her feet as she spots me, hurrying around the counter until she's standing right in front of me. Taking me by the hand, she gives my fingers a squeeze.

"I'm so sorry," she says. "But she's gone."

My legs threaten to go out from under me. I widen my stance, thoughts reeling. I knew I shouldn't have left her here unprotected. I should have known that they'd get to her somehow.

"She's dead?" I ask. "How?"

The nurse gives me a sheepish look. "No, not dead. Just gone. She took off sometime during the graveyard shift."

"But I don't understand. Didn't she just have major surgery?"

The nurse nods. Obviously not concerned with patient privacy under the circumstances, she admits, "They removed her spleen."

"Then how could they just release her after that?"

"They didn't. She snuck out."

My head throbs to the frantic beat of my heart, my anxiety levels rising. "How can you be sure that somebody didn't come in here and take her?"

The nurse looks at me like I'm crazy. And maybe I am. But not about this. I'm fairly certain that I'm acting appropriately, given what's happened.

"Call your head of security up here." When the nurse doesn't move, I pull my badge out of my purse and hold it out to her. "Now," I command. I feel bad for being rude, but each passing second carries the answers I need further away.

She scurries back behind her desk to make the call, leaving me pacing the hallway, drawing stares from patients and visitors until the man from yesterday arrives. He doesn't look pleased to see me again so soon. I'm about to cement that feeling in him.

"Have you called the police?" I ask, struggling not to shout.

"No. Why?"

"I told you yesterday that she was in danger. And you promised me your staff would make sure that no one would get on this floor who wasn't supposed to."

"They didn't."

"How can you be sure?"

Despite it appearing to be the last thing he wants to

do, he gestures for me to follow him, leading the way to the elevators. The ride back to the ground floor is tense, neither of us breaking the silence. He drums his fingers against the railing bolted along the polished back wall until he catches the look I'm giving him.

Clearing his throat, he darts through the doors as soon as they open, hurrying across the waxed floor so quickly his shoes squeak. I trail behind him, trying to keep my temper in check. But it's easier to be angry than scared. Especially when I find myself back in the small office where we'd sat watching the video of my attack just twenty-four hours before.

Though the feed on the monitors shows real-time footage, when I look at them, I see the man in the white mask, black hoodie, and flashy shoes. A burlap sack being pulled over my head. The impacts that caused every one of the lumps and bumps and bruises my body bears today. I sit in a chair before one is offered, worried that my legs will fail to support me much longer.

Wordlessly, the security guard takes the seat beside me and taps on one of the keyboards. An image of the floor we were just on appears on one of the screens. The woman comes into view. She stumbles down the hall, trailing her hand along the wall for support, limping. And alone.

We watch as she ducks into a room. According to the timestamp running in the corner, several minutes pass before she comes back out, this time wearing stolen clothes. We follow her progress, one angle ceding to another as she makes her way out of the hospital. Just as she's leaving, she looks directly at the security camera above the door.

Her eyes shine. Her mouth contorts into a grimace. But more than in pain, she appears terrified. The guard pauses the footage as I lean closer to the screen. Maybe it's because she's conscious, but here in this frame, more than ever, something about her strikes me as eerily familiar.

"Do you trust me now?" he asks.

I don't, and I'm sure the look I give him says as much. But I do believe him. There was no sign of anyone coercing her. The woman left of her own accord.

"Can you email me a copy of the video?"

"I'm not so sure I should do that. It was one thing yesterday…"

"You mean when I was violently attacked on hospital grounds?"

He clears his throat but doesn't answer.

"And now the woman I told you was in trouble left. She did it on her own—"

"Exactly!"

"But I fail to see how that makes it any better. Because the hospital staff failed to notice that an obviously injured woman basically dragged herself through the front doors. Care to explain to me how that happened?"

"We can't force a patient to stay against their will."

"Still, there are certain protocols that need to be followed when a patient is discharged, are there not? At the very least, a waiver releasing the hospital of any liability from complications that arise from going against doctor's orders?"

I wasn't sure if I was being too vague, but the defeated nod he gives me lets me know that it was enough. My implications are clear. That woman could be lying dead somewhere right now—and in the eyes of the law, or at least the media and, as such, public scrutiny— the hospital would be to blame.

"Same email as yesterday?" he asks.

"Yes. Thank you."

I almost feel bad for the man as I stand to leave. But not quite.

Because I have more important things to be concerned with. Like what's going on. It's obvious that the woman was afraid. Yet all she had to do was speak to someone here and they would have called the police for her. She probably even could have done it herself from her room.

But she hadn't. Instead, she chose to leave. Why? And perhaps just as important—where was she going in her condition, on foot?

CHAPTER 21

I have to figure out who the woman is. It's the only way to find her, to get her the help she needs before it's too late. But what if it's too late already?

It looked like someone had hurt her well before they rammed her headfirst into a tree, and whoever it was, they scared her badly enough that she left the hospital as soon as she could drag herself out the door.

Obviously, she's in danger. And so I am. But is it from the same source?

Sweat dampens my clothes as I walk a big loop around the hospital, looking for any trace of the woman, but there's nothing. No clue where she went. No signs of a struggle.

But she couldn't have gotten far, not on her own. Had she called someone from her room before she left? If she had, I suspect that it's going to take more than my threats to go public to get the hospital to release that kind of information.

I sigh, frustrated. This is useless. I'm just wasting my time. I should go home.

A faint noise draws my attention. I come to a stop, holding my breath, trying to place it. Feel a flash of disappointment when I realize that it's not the miracle clue I was hoping for, but my phone. Fishing it out of my purse, I glance at the screen, intending to ignore it. But I change my mind when I see the number.

"Hello?"

"Hey, girl."

My pulse quickens as a drop of hope mixes with the despair inside me. "Hi, Mallory."

"Is now a good time to talk?"

"It's perfect," I say. I start making my way around the hospital again, this time looking for cameras on any of the surrounding businesses and houses.

"Great. I got the paint samples you sent. The lab said we can expect the results sometime next week."

The hope I'd felt vanishes. That's too long.

"But I found a possible match for the vehicle."

"You—wait. What? You did?"

"Uh-huh. A white Toyota Tundra was reported stolen by Dade County police three months ago. They found it abandoned in a shipping warehouse parking lot at a marina a week later."

"Oh."

If they recovered the truck, then it can't possibly be the one that Jane Doe was driving.

"Yeah, but get this. They seized it and had it towed, but when they sent a crew out to process the vehicle for evidence, they couldn't find it."

"What do you mean?"

"I mean it disappeared from the impound lot. Poof. Vanished."

"How does that happen?"

"Well, they're still trying to figure that out, because it's not supposed to. Especially considering that the only people who can access the vehicles kept there are the police..."

"It was an inside job."

"Either that, or someone was paid to look the other way. Both equate to the same thing, though."

A dirty cop. No wonder the mystery woman was so scared. She didn't know who she could trust. But how had she come to be in possession of the vehicle?

"Tell her about Jane Doe's prints." I can just barely hear the voice in the background.

"Oh, yeah," Mallory says.

"Is that Director Jacobson?" I ask.

"It is. I filled her in on the accident. She submitted the request to the Miami field office for the magneto-optical test I was telling you about."

"Can I talk to her?"

"Sure."

A series of muffled noises sound in my ear as the phone changes hands. And then, "Agent Knox?"

"Yes, ma'am."

"What I wanted Agent Chan to tell you was that I just spoke with the local police down there, and there seems to be some confusion about Jane Doe's fingerprints. An officer took them when she was released from surgery to see if they could figure out her identity."

"Did they get a match?"

"They did. To a woman in Coral Gables."

"So they know who she is?"

"That's just it. When they sent someone to her last known address, hoping to find next of kin, they found the woman herself."

"Was there some kind of mistake?"

"I don't think it was a mistake at all. The Coral Gable woman's prints are in the system because she's a teacher. They were electronically scanned when she was initially hired, then again when she changed school districts several years ago. But the ones on file now are no longer a match to hers. I think someone purposely switched Jane Doe's prints with someone else's so they'd be attached to a different identity."

It's the second indicator that a dirty cop could be involved. It makes this whole situation even more dangerous. Because if it's true, then someone has the same tools and information at their disposal that we do.

"There's an officer on the way to the hospital now with a warrant. I was hoping you could be there when they draw the blood. I've requested a sample for our lab to conduct a DNA analysis."

"I'm there now. It's too late," I say. "She's gone."

I wonder if the hospital has a sample of Jane Doe's blood that we could use. Wouldn't they have had to run labs for her surgery?

"Did the hospital release her?"

"No. She dragged herself out the front door overnight."

"And no one stopped her?"

"I don't think anyone noticed. And there's more."

"Tell me everything."

"It's a long story."

"That's fine, Cassidy. Just start at the beginning."

"It all began with the break-in."

"You thought that wasn't related to what happened before. The people who wanted your grandfather's property."

"I didn't. I still don't. But I do think that it has something to do with this woman and the crash."

"How so?"

I fill her in on how I suspect that a second vehicle was involved in the wreck. And how I think the woman had been beaten and tortured beforehand. Then, drawing a deep breath, I tell her about the attack in the parking garage.

"Are you okay?"

"Yes. But I got lucky. Very lucky. I'm not sure what his intentions were, but he tried pulling a hood over my head."

Director Jacobson curses.

"I fought him. When I got the upper hand, he ran away."

"When was this?"

"Yesterday morning."

"Next time, Agent Knox, I expect you to inform me immediately. When someone attacks one of my own, I want to know about it."

"Yes, ma'am."

"And you think the attack had something to do with this woman?"

"I can't be sure, but my gut says that it does. Either way, he was one of the people who broke into my house."

She inhales sharply. Her voice is tense as she asks, "Are you positive?"

"I am."

"How?"

"I compared footage from my security camera to the footage from the hospital. Same build. Same mask. Same shoes."

"Do you think they followed you to the hospital?"

"I think they were already there. I think they were trying to keep me from talking with the woman."

"The woman who we can't identify. And now that she's gone, she can't tell you who she is."

"Exactly."

Director Jacobson mutters to herself. Then she asks me, "I'm assuming since you said she dragged herself out of the hospital, that you saw video of this?"

"Yes."

"How banged up is her face?"

"Some cuts and swelling, nothing major."

"Do you have a copy of the footage?"

"I do."

"Good. Send it over. I'll have it run through a facial recognition program, see if we can't find out her identity that way."

"Thank you," I whisper. I want to tell her how scared I am. How relieved I am to have her help. But I don't think I can get the words out. My breathing is shaky and weak, but it has nothing to do with having just finished my second circuit around the hospital with still no clue of where the woman disappeared to.

"I want you to be very careful, Agent Knox. Whatever's going on, they have someone on the inside."

I nod though she can't see me, still not trusting myself to speak.

"Is there anyone there you trust?"

"Only Jake," I say.

"I don't suppose he's in law enforcement? Or has any military training?"

"No. He's a lawyer."

She groans. "Where are you now?"

"I'm still at the hospital."

"Send me the video for facial recognition, then get home. I want you to hole up and sit tight. I'm going to make some calls and see how fast the Miami field office can send someone to assist. I'll call as soon as I work things out on my end. In the meantime, let me know if anything else happens."

I jog across the lot, locking myself in the car before we end the call. On the one hand, I know I should feel relieved to have help on the horizon. On the other, it feels like a blow to my already fragile ego, that I wasn't able to deal with this myself. I failed.

But at least I'm still here, able to have that as a concern. Because I'm starting to suspect that whoever is after me would prefer to have it otherwise.

CHAPTER 22

Time is an odd thing. There's never enough of it. But even when it feels like it's running out, somehow each individual minute can seem to pass incredibly slowly, especially when you're waiting, like I am now.

Because I can't shake the sensation that something bad is coming. Something worse than what's already happened.

I know I need to try to prepare, but the truth is, I have no idea where to start. So I'm doing whatever I can.

Even though I'm far from finishing the home improvement projects I've already started, I stopped by the hardware store on my way home. Both doors are now reinforced with metal screens over the glass panes. I used enough U-nails to attach them that I'm fairly convinced it would take a cannonball to remove them.

Despite that, I find myself sitting on the floor in the middle of Butch's room with my computer balanced on my lap because it feels safer back here. Less vulnerable. And despite knowing that I should be pulling up the carpet so I can lay the new flooring down, I can't stop staring at a still shot of Jane Doe instead.

"What are you doing?"

My gaze tears from the woman's face with a Velcro-like rip and darts to Jake. Something about the way he's leaning against the doorframe, shirt sleeves rolled up to his elbows, one foot crossed over the other as he watches me—it's just so relaxed. So casual.

I feel a pang of regret as I try to remember the last time anything I did was so carefree. It's exhausting, always being on edge. The fear, the worry, the guilt—the weight of it is overwhelming.

It makes me want to scream. To throw caution to the wind, go outside, and yell a challenge to whoever these people are at the top of my lungs. To just get it over with already. Instead, I can't even bring myself to sit in the kitchen or living room right now because it makes me feel too nervous.

If I can't even keep myself safe, how can I expect to protect Jake? I promised myself that I would never put him in harm's way again. I can't deny it any longer—the situation has gotten too dangerous. It would be selfish to keep holding on. My heart spasms in my chest as I realize that the time has come for me to force myself to let him go.

"I was too late when I got to the hospital today."

"What do you mean 'too late?'" he asks with a frown.

"The woman was gone. She left."

"They let her go?"

"No. She took off on her own."

"Wasn't she too injured for that?"

I nod. "But she did it anyway. Something has her that scared, Jake, that she literally dragged herself out of the hospital in the middle of the night. I should have done something to make her feel safer. Done more to help her."

"There's no way you could have known she'd leave like that. And she could have asked someone there for help. You can't blame yourself."

And yet I do. I can't help it.

"Maybe it's for the best," he continues.

"She could barely walk."

"You can't save everyone, Cassie."

"I feel like I can't save anyone."

Including myself, though I don't say it out loud. And I can't expect him to understand what that means. How it makes me feel. The way it makes me question every action, from walking across a parking lot on my own to something as simple as sitting on the couch in the living room. Or what it means for us.

"No one ever said you had to," Jake says. He comes over and squats in front of me. Rests his hands gently on my knees. "You're amazing just the way you are. The only one who expects you to be a superhero is you. And all this pressure you put on yourself, it's not healthy."

"It's too dangerous for you to stay here."

"If that's true, you're coming with me."

"I can't, Jake. I'm the one they're after. We need—" My voice catches. I draw a deep, shaky breath. "I think we should take a break."

"You don't mean that."

"I can't be the reason you get hurt again."

"And you can't make decisions for me, Cassie. You can't push me away just because you're scared."

I ignore his words, hoping that seeing her fear will put some sense into him. Restarting the clip I had on pause, the one where she looks at the camera with an expression of pure terror before she walks out the door, I turn the screen toward Jake. He bends his head for a closer look.

"What am I looking at? Who is that?"

"That's the woman who was in the accident. The Jane Doe. You don't recognize her?"

"Her face was covered with blood. And I was busy trying to open the door. Then, once you climbed inside the truck, all I could think about was whether it was safe for you to be in there or not."

But there's something about his expression that tells me there's something he's not saying. I watch as he sinks the rest of the way to the floor and pulls the laptop to him. Runs a hand through his hair, leaving it standing on end as he touches the screen, pausing the clip.

"There's something familiar about her," I say, moving to sit beside him. "I can't shake the feeling that I know her somehow."

I hear his jaw pop as it clenches. When I glance over at him, he's gone pale. A vein appears along the center of his forehead.

"Jake?"

When he doesn't respond, I put a hand on his shoulder. Finally, his eyes lift from the screen to meet mine, a stricken look on his face.

"Is everything okay?" I ask, though I find that I'm afraid to hear his answer. Because I know it's not. That much is obvious.

Something is very, very wrong. But what he says? It's the last thing I expect.

"Cassie." His lips tremble. He swallows hard. His eyes glisten, voice wavering as he says, "I think that might be my mom."

CHAPTER 23

I can't feel the floor under my feet as I pace up and down the hallway. It's gone. Not literally, of course, but that thing that was once beneath me, holding me up? It's vanished.

Now, I feel myself dangling over a precipice that threatens to swallow me whole. It's not the first time I've been here. I've fought my way back from the edge once before. The difference is, this time, I'm not alone.

Reaching the end of my path, I glance through the bedroom doorway to where Jake is still sitting on the floor, the computer cradled in his lap as he stares at the screen. I force myself to turn away, hurrying my steps until I'm back in the living room before I speak.

"That's right. Janine Walker," I confirm for Director Jacobson. "She left town over thirty years ago. As far as I know, she hasn't been seen or heard from since."

I wish I could ask Jake to confirm that, even though I know it's true. Jake's reaction is proof enough.

"And how did you know her?"

"She and my mom were best friends. She took off right after my parents died in a car crash."

"Cassidy." Director Jacobson's voice is soft. Too soft. Yet something about it is deafening inside my head. "Part of what we do when we vet new recruits is look into their backgrounds. A lot of agents choose this field because of crimes that happened in their past."

I swallow hard, sinking down onto the arm of the couch. Director Jacobson isn't one to go off on tangents. If she's telling me this, there's a reason. And I know I need to brace myself for whatever it is.

"As long as the prospects are grounded and stable and don't appear to have any kind of vendetta, we're fine with it. It keeps them motivated. Makes them better agents even, because they've been in the shoes of the victims and their families. It helps them handle cases more sensitively."

I can't take it anymore. Worried I might go insane before she makes her point, I interrupt.

"With all due respect, ma'am, what's that got to do with what's going on now?"

Director Jacobson clears her throat.

"I'm sorry. I thought you knew."

"Knew what?"

My body starts to quiver, responding to fear, the source of which is still unknown.

"I'm not sure how to tell you this, but your parents weren't killed in a car crash."

"What?" If I felt ungrounded before, now I feel adrift in space. But surely she's mistaken. "That's impossible. My grandfather told me. He said an animal must have darted out into the road in front of them. Why would he lie?"

"That I can't tell you. Perhaps it was because you were so young when it happened. Maybe it seemed easier. Or kinder. But whatever his reason, the story he told you wasn't the truth. Your parents were killed in a home invasion."

The rush of the ocean fills my skull, like I've just pressed a seashell to my ear. I can feel the blood draining from my head. It leaves a strange numb sensation in its place.

All the survival skills Butch taught me. Had there been a reason for them? One beyond a man trying to prepare his only granddaughter for life in a dangerous world?

I have so many questions. Too many. But only one makes it past my lips.

"Where was I?" When an answer doesn't come, I repeat it, louder, more insistent. "Marla, where was I when this happened?"

Director Jacobson clears her throat. "If I recall correctly, according to the report, you were spending the night at a friend's house."

There's only one friend I remember from back then. I glance down the hallway, lowering my voice as I ask, "Which friend?"

"It's been a long time since I read the file, Agent Knox."

"Was it the Walkers' house?"

There's a beat of silence, and then, "I believe it might have been."

What does it all mean? Is there a connection between my parents' murders and Jake's mom's disappearance?

"Cassidy?"

"Yeah?"

My voice sounds wooden and hollow, unlike my own.

"Are you okay?"

"Yes." I'm not sure if I really am, but I know it's the answer I should give. "Can you send me everything you have on my parents' case?"

"I'm not sure if that's a—"

"Please?"

The desperation in my voice must be clear, because

she agrees, albeit reluctantly.

"I'll email it first thing when I get to the office in the morning."

The comment makes me pull the phone away from my ear to check the time. It's almost seven. She must be at home, and she was kind enough to answer. Again.

But I'm going to have to put an end to this dependency on her—she's too kind to do it herself. Soon, she won't be my boss anymore. Even now, it's only a technicality.

"And you should know I was able to confirm that the Miami field office is sending an agent to help. Special Agent Richards. He just wrapped up the case he was working on. He should arrive tomorrow."

I search my mind, trying to recall the conversation, the reason. That's right. I'd called her when I first discovered that the woman—that Janine—had fled from the hospital. Could that really have been earlier today? It seems so long ago now.

"I'll see if I can't find a DMV photo of Janine Walker to use as a comparison against the footage you sent me earlier, too. See if the facial recognition program confirms they're a match."

"Thank you."

"Everything's going to be all right, Cassidy. You know that, don't you?"

"Yes. Thank you, Director Jacobson. I appreciate all your help."

"Of course. We'll talk soon. Goodnight."

"Goodnight."

It feels like the last bit of solid footing I'd been holding onto has crumbled. I force myself to stand anyway. Because this really doesn't change anything for me. Car accident or murder, my parents are still dead. They aren't coming back.

But Jake's mom? She's still alive. Or, at least, she was when she left the hospital last night. But if I don't find her, and soon, there's no guarantee how long she's going to stay that way.

CHAPTER 24

There are moments in your life where everything changes. I know this is one of mine. I can either allow myself to fall to pieces, or I can pull myself together and be there for the man I love. The same man with whom I'm falling in love. The one who now seems as entangled in this mess as I am.

As relieved as I am that this revelation came before I did anything to irreparably damage our relationship, I find myself faced with a new challenge. What does our future hold if I can't do this for him? Not just support him in his time of need, the way he's supported me, but do everything in my power to help him find his mom before it's too late.

Because if the situation were reversed? I know he'd do everything he could to help.

I want—no, I *need*—to be the version of myself I see reflected back at me when I look into his eyes. So, straightening my spine, rolling my shoulders back, lifting my head tall, I try to project confidence as I stride down the hall and into Butch's room, where I find him still staring blankly at his mother's image on the screen.

"Jake, don't worry. We'll find her. We'll keep her safe."

He sets the laptop to the side and gets to his feet.

"I'm not sure we should."

My stomach lurches. A lump rises in my throat.

"What do you mean?" I ask warily. "She's your mother. We have to do anything we can to help her. Don't you think?"

He swallows hard. It hurts me to see the anguish in his expression, a physical ache that makes me want to take him in my arms and soothe his pain. "I just want you to be careful, okay?"

"Yeah, of course. But I can do both. Be careful and find her. Director Jacobson is sending a field agent to help. He should be here—"

Jake's shaking his head. "Maybe it's for the best if she stays gone."

My heart beats faster in my chest. "What makes you say that?"

"Because she left me, Cassie."

I remind myself that he doesn't know about what really happened to my parents. About the danger his mom might have been in. And now's not the time to tell him.

"Maybe she had to go."

"And did she *have* to leave me behind?"

"Jake, I remember enough about your mom to know that she adored you."

He snorts. "She had a strange way of showing it."

My throat squeezes so tight I can barely breathe. I can't deny that a part of me hates Janine Walker a bit right now, no matter her reason for leaving, for the simple fact that she hurt Jake so badly. But at the same time, hadn't I planned on doing the same thing, in a way? Removing him from my life to keep him out of harm's way?

"It might not have been safe for you to go with her," I say, desperate to make him feel better, to make this right. "You were eight."

"And I'm forty-one now. So where has she been all these years? Do you really believe that in all that time, she couldn't come back to see me once?"

"Maybe she really couldn't," I choke out.

"Or maybe she didn't want to face the kid she abandoned with an abusive drunk. She knew what he was like. Knew how bitter he was about knocking up his girlfriend in high school and getting saddled with a family he didn't want so early in life. She had to have known how he'd react when he got stuck raising that kid on his own."

I remember seeing the bruises on his face in high school. I've noticed the faint scars still etched across his back. And I'm well aware that the visible injuries aren't the worst ones he suffered.

"Did you know that until now, I thought my dad must have killed her? It was the only explanation I could come up with for why she could have possibly left me with someone like him. All these years I've suspected him of being a murderer. I baited him, even, trying to get him to kill me, too, hoping he might finally face justice. But it turns out he was the better parent, because at least he stuck around."

Tears sting my eyes, heat my skin as they trail down my cheeks. "I'm sorry," I say, cupping my hand against his cheek. "You shouldn't have had to go through that."

He takes my hand in his, kisses my palm and says, "Just promise me you won't let your guard down. Not until this is all over."

"I promise."

Then his lips are against mine, soft at first, but the kisses grow harder, more urgent. I wrap my arms around his neck, hands threading through his hair as he grips me by my hips, drawing me closer, his fingertips hot against my skin as they edge under the hem of my shirt, trailing up along my sides as he lifts the material over my head.

I step backward, pulling him with me until my spine is against the wall. I press the brand seared into my flesh against the hard surface until the throb becomes so excruciating that my mind goes blessedly blank.

I've become used to the pain. But not the shame of bearing the mark of a killer on my body. And though my first instinct was panic at the thought of Jake finally seeing the mark, now a new sensation has taken hold.

I feel like I'm being devoured. It's intoxicating, being needed this badly. I want this. Want him. I crave the way he silences the static in my head.

Only, not like this.

This isn't about the two of us. It's about drowning out the loudness of his thoughts, the hurt he feels from being abandoned. My hands drop to his, stilling his movements as he fumbles with the button on my shorts.

"Jake."

He freezes. Takes a giant step away from me. He looks absolutely mortified.

"I'm sorry," he says.

"No. Don't be."

"I just… I can't think straight right now. If it's her, if it's true…"

When he doesn't continue, I move forward, closing the distance he's put between us. Smile despite the way my skin tightens as I expose my scarred back to the air. Rising on my toes, I press my lips against his.

"You deserve better," he says against my kiss.

It's not true.

"And so do you."

"No, I mean you deserve someone who doesn't have so much baggage."

I laugh. "Have you met me? You're the one I want, Jake Walker. You always have been. And I want all of you. The sunshine and the storms."

But would he want me if he knew how close I'd come to pushing him away?

He wraps his arms tight around me, lowering his head to my shoulder, burying his face in my neck. I squeeze him just as hard, holding him until the tension in his body eases, his muscles ticking like a cooling engine. Then he straightens, clears his throat.

Won't look at me as he says, "I need some air. I'm going to take a walk."

"Do you want me to come?"

He shakes his head, still not meeting my eyes. "I think it's best if I'm alone right now."

I watch him go, feeling helpless. Wishing that there was something I could do to take away his pain. To take back every time I considered abandoning him for any reason. And desperately hoping that this separation between us isn't as permanent as it feels.

CHAPTER 25

It's hard to breathe. I feel gutted. But I'm not sure which recent injury to my psyche has wounded me worse.

Discovering that the story I believed for the last thirty-three years about my parents' deaths was a lie, and that they were actually murdered? Or knowing that I'm the reason Jake's in so much pain right now.

If only I had let the mystery surrounding Jane Doe drop, then none of this would have happened. Jake wouldn't be experiencing renewed anguish over being abandoned by his mom. And I wouldn't be dealing with the guilt of causing his pain—or the heartache of my own. Because I can't stop agonizing over why Butch lied to me all these years, even after I was grown and became an FBI agent.

Had he thought I was too weak to handle it? I can't let myself believe that. I won't. Now more than ever I need to summon the strong woman he raised me to be.

Doing my best to stay distracted, I sit on the couch, sorting through the box of mementoes I'd found in Butch's room, but looking through them brings a pain of its own. Photos of my parents, who I can barely remember. Pictures of Butch, now also gone. And shots of me and Jake as children.

I hold one such image in my hand, drinking in every

detail. In it, Jake and I are sitting next to each other. He's still a toddler and I'm just a baby. Jake has a chubby arm thrown around me, his lips pressed to my cheek in a kiss. My face is completely filled by a huge smile, impressive given the size of my massive head.

It's always been the two of us. I can't believe how close I came to destroying that.

Swallowing at the lump making my throat tight, I check the time. Set the photograph back in the box and stand. I know I need to give Jake space, but his absence makes me uneasy. If I can just put my eyes on him, I'll feel better.

I scan the property as I step outside, but he's nowhere in sight. I thought maybe he'd be bedding the animals down for the night, a task we both find strangely relaxing, but a glance at the paddock lets me know that's not true. Daisy, the zebra, nickers when she sees me, leading her foal toward the barn. The mule and the cow follow.

The zebra detours toward me as I approach the fence. Daisy's velvet soft nose brushes against my cheek, her head a heavy weight on my shoulder as she stretches to reach my hair. Closing my eyes, I breathe in her scent, rubbing my palm against her neck until she tires of playing with the end of my braid and withdraws, continuing the trek toward her dinner bucket.

As she leaves, Stephano frolics over to me. The mini goat's jumping skills make it impossible to keep him contained, but he usually stays close to the other animals—unless there's a human nearby. The little guy craves constant attention.

"I'm surprised you're not keeping Jake company right now," I tell him as I stoop to rub the skin at the base of his horns the way he likes. When I stop, he circles around my feet like a cat, butting my legs gently with his head until I pick him up.

I scratch his rough coat as I carry him to the barn. Open the paddock gate, herding everyone into their stalls. Check their water and give them a meal for the night. But still, there's no sign of Jake.

Grabbing a banana from the tack room, I feed half to each of the pigs, Chip and Bagel, then put the peel inside a treat ball intended for dogs and give it to Stephano, knowing it's the only thing that will keep him entertained while I make my getaway. Then, pulling on a disposable glove, I take a roaster chicken from the fridge and hike out to the pond out back.

I was young when Chomp came to the sanctuary. Young enough that it was a shock to discover that there were people out there who were cruel enough to do something as horrible as removing an alligator's top jaw with a snare, then leave him like that to suffer and die.

But I was also old enough to see and appreciate the people on the other end of the spectrum, good people like Butch who cared for the sick and injured creatures that needed help. To my child's mind, his efforts made the bad in the world seem not so scary.

Tears burn my eyes as I long for my grandfather, wishing he was here with me now. He'd know what to do. How to make things better. Or at the very least, he could tell me why he lied.

Reaching the pond, I toss the chicken to Chomp, the gator now over thirteen feet long, much older and bigger than most of his species live to be. It just goes to show that sometimes intervening is a good thing. Which is why I need to find Jake. Whether he wants to talk or not, he shouldn't be going through what he's feeling right now alone.

When I didn't see him walking along the paddock, I really thought I'd find him out here. Maybe he passed by while I was in the barn, and he's already returned to the house.

Crickets have started their evening song by the time I make it back to the front of the property. The only other sound is the crunch of my steps on the dry grass. And though it's a noise that I've heard thousands of times during my life, tonight there's something eerie about it.

I try to push down the feeling of foreboding that's wrapped around me, but it's grabbed on too tightly. And as something glints in the driveway ahead of me, caught by the last rays of light cast by the dying day, I have a sickening feeling that I'm about to find out why.

I hurry up the drive for a closer look, but once I can tell what the object is, I stumble to a sudden halt. My feet refuse to keep moving as I stare at what I've found. There, only ten feet ahead of me, lies a phone.

The screen of the device isn't just cracked, it's shattered, as if someone took their heel and purposely broke it. The dirt around it is turned up, like there's been a struggle. And flecks of something dark that I'm trying to convince myself isn't blood stain the pale earth around it.

The trembling starts in my chest, spreading outward until my entire body shakes violently. My heart beats frantically as I struggle to breathe. Though my lungs refuse to cooperate, I force the last of the air from them in a strangled sound as I gasp Jake's name.

I feel my eyes widening until they're too big for my head. They grow dry from lack of blinking. But I can't look away. I can't risk missing anything. The stakes are too high. And night is falling fast.

"Jake," I call again, louder this time, more desperate, unable to keep the fear from my voice.

Breaking into a run, I skirt around the disturbance, unwilling yet to think of it as a crime scene, and race across the grass alongside the driveway until I reach the road. Blink the tears from my eyes, but it doesn't change the truth—there's nothing visible in either direction.

I tell myself that I'm just being paranoid as I sprint to the house, bursting inside with such force that the door slams against the wall behind it and swings back against me, knocking me off balance.

"Jake?" My voice grows hoarse as I yell his name, searching every room. But there's no response. And no sign of Jake.

I can't deny it any longer. Tears stream silently down my cheeks as I grab a Ziploc bag from a drawer in the kitchen, eyes snagging on Jake's keys on the table. His briefcase on one of the chairs, suit jacket draped over the back. Fighting the urge to bury my nose in the fabric to inhale his scent while I have a chance, before it disappears, I find a flashlight and go back outside.

I light my path, making my way carefully to Jake's phone, trying not to step where any shoe tread is visible in the dirt. Slipping the bag over my hand, I pick up the device by its edges and seal it inside. Take pictures of the shoe impressions. Then call Director Jacobson, not knowing—or caring—what time it is.

"Agent Knox?"

"They took him."

"Took who?"

"Jake."

"Janine Walker's son? That Jake?"

"Yes."

"Same last name?"

"Yes."

"Are you sure? Are you positive there's no way he could have left on his own?"

I turn to look at his truck still parked in front of the house behind me. Think of his keys on the table—he couldn't get into his condo without them. And he hadn't changed when he came home from work. He was still in dress shoes. We're miles from the nearest house.

"Yes," I say. "I'm sure. I found his phone smashed in the driveway. It looks like there'd been a struggle."

Director Jacobson curses.

"Are you all right? Do you have anyone you can call to be with you right now?"

I have the same answer for both questions. "No."

"Hold tight. I'm going to call Agent Richards. He's the one who's supposed to help you tomorrow. I'll see if he can push that up and make the drive tonight. But, Cassidy, I need to know. Do you have any idea who we're dealing with here? Or why they'd take your friend?"

I know why she's asking. It's infinitely easier to solve a crime when you have a suspect, or at the very least, a motive. But I don't know anything about these people besides the one thing that I wish I didn't—that they don't hesitate to use violence.

My stomach twists into knots, my voice cracking as I say, "No. I wish I did."

"If there's something you haven't told me… it's okay. We'll find a way to deal with it."

"The only thing I haven't told you is that I love him."

I keep the second part of the statement to myself—*and that I'll do anything to get him back.* Because it's true. I'll burn this entire swamp to the ground if that's what it takes to find him. And that makes me a liability the Bureau can't afford to have.

Director Jacobson exhales heavily into the phone. "Just stay positive, Cassidy. Help is on the way."

Ending the call, I sink to my knees beside the signs of a scuffle in the dirt. It's the only evidence I have. The only clue to go on.

Tracking the steps of each shoe pattern, I study the impressions until a choreography of the attack emerges in my mind. Stare at them until my vision goes hazy. Until darkness falls and I can't see the four distinct treads anymore.

It was three against one. In his injured condition, Jake didn't stand a chance.

CHAPTER 26

The darkness has started to fade back to light by the time Agent Richards arrives. I'm still sitting in the driveway, keeping watch over the shoe prints. Guarding what feels like the only connection I have to Jake right now.

The headlights of the black SUV turn off when they hit me, the vehicle inching closer until it rolls to a stop several yards away. A man with neatly combed hair wearing a navy polo shirt with the FBI logo tucked into a pair of khakis emerges from within. He eyes me for a moment before approaching cautiously with the handle of a heavy-duty, oversized box gripped in one hand.

"Special Agent Richards," he says, introducing himself.

"Cassidy Knox."

"Sorry it took me so long. I had to stop on the way to pick up some supplies. Your director said there are some shoe prints we need to cast?"

I point in front of me.

He swipes the air around him as the mosquitoes descend. Defends himself from a bite with a painful sounding slap. "Geez, they're relentless, aren't they? Have you been sitting out here all night?"

"Yes."

"Aren't you getting eaten alive?"

I shrug, not bothering to tell him I've gone numb.

"Well, we'll wait until the sun's up to take the casts."

"No, let's do it now." I gesture toward the house. "You can mix up the plaster in there. Use whatever you need."

"You mind if I make a pot of coffee while I'm at it?"

"Do whatever you've got to do." Then, thinking of the dark splotches on the dirt, I ask, "Did you bring any phenolphthalein with you?"

He snaps open the clasp on his supply box, removes what he needs and points to the rest of it. "Help yourself."

Pulling myself to my feet, I riffle around. Withdraw a sterile swab and remove it from its outer packaging. Roll it across one of the spots I fear is blood and hold my breath as I add a drop of phenolphthalein and some hydrogen peroxide.

A whimper escapes me as the tip turns pink, confirming my suspicions. Though the Kastle-Meyer test isn't definitive, I know that it's likely not a false positive. What I don't know is whether I should hope that it isn't Jake's blood, or that it is. Because if he made one of his attackers bleed, chances are they paid him back tenfold.

My throat is painfully tight, unshed tears making the back of my nose burn as I busy myself with finding the best angle for the flashlight to capture the prints so we can see to take the casts. That's what I'm doing when Agent Richards returns.

"You really think this is going to give us a lead?" he asks as he hands me the Tupperware container he used to mix the Plaster of Paris in.

"It has to," I say, spooning the mixture over the impressions. "Right now, it's all we've got to go on. And one of the guys involved in all this wears some ridiculously expensive shoes. I want to know if any of these prints belong to him."

His eyebrows arch. "We already have a suspect? How's that?"

"Some people broke into my house a couple nights ago. Thanks to his fancy shoes, I know that one of them was the same person who later attacked me in a hospital parking garage. So for one, whatever they're after, they haven't gotten it yet, and for two, kidnapping appears to be part of their MO."

"Fair enough. And this guy that's gone missing? Jake Walker? He was your boyfriend?"

I find myself rankled by Agent Richards' use of the past tense.

"Is. He *is* my boyfriend."

He watches me in silence as I continue filling the impressions with the plaster, using the back of the spoon to gently press the mixture into the grooves and smooth out any air bubbles.

Standing, I look down at my handiwork, wondering if I can find enough extension cords to run a fan out here to quicken the drying time. Grabbing Jake's bagged cell phone and Agent Richards' field kit, I start toward the house to check.

"Sorry. I didn't mean to upset you," he says as he falls into step beside me and takes the toolbox from my hand.

I cut a sharp look his way. Sigh deeply as I force myself to soften it. It's not his fault that this is happening. He's here to help. Drove through the night to get here. I should be grateful.

"No, I'm sorry. I'm just… worried."

"That's understandable."

I give him a forced smile as I open the door for him.

"Tell me what I can do to help," he says, leading the way to the kitchen. He sets his box on the floor next to the table.

"You any good at lifting prints?" I ask. Holding Jake's phone up, I tilt it to catch the light. Despite the shattered screen, I can see three distinct fingertip-sized circles. Pulling out my own phone, I press the power button to illuminate the lockscreen and compare them.

"Not to brag, but I hold my own against the techs. You want me to dust his phone?"

"Yeah. In a sec."

One of the circles on Jake's phone matches where the biometric sensor is onscreen. But if his cell is anything like mine, it doesn't always work. After washing my hands, restarting it, or sometimes, I suspect, just to be difficult, it makes me enter my four-digit code.

Swiping up, I override the biometric sensor on my phone, making the numbers for the option to enter a PIN appear. One of the circles on Jake's phone corresponds to the two. The other matches the seven.

"We've got people back at the office who can usually find a way to gain access, if that's what you're after," Agent Richards volunteers.

Swallowing hard, I say, "I don't think that will be necessary."

"You know his passcode?"

"I can wager a guess."

He arches his eyebrows at me, waiting.

"He uses the two and the seven," I say.

"Okay. So we just try every combination of those two numbers until we get it right."

"No need. It's two-two-seven-seven."

"I thought you said you didn't know it?"

"I don't. But I do know the numbers that correspond to my name. Two-two-seven-seven. C-A-S-S." Holding the phone out to him, I say, "We can test my theory after you print it."

"You two must be close," he says as he takes it from me and sets it on the kitchen table. Opening his field kit, he removes a pair of disposable nitrile gloves, fingerprint powder, a brush, a roll of clear tape, and a stack of backing cards. Taking a seat, he slips the gloves on and opens the Ziploc.

My voice wavers as I say, "Yes."

"Anyone besides the two of you know that?"

"What do you mean?"

"Is it public knowledge that you're an item?"

"I mean, we haven't advertised it, but it isn't a secret, either. Why?"

"When I was driving in, it looked like this was a pretty big place. You've got a lot of land here, don't you?" he asks, setting the phone on top of the baggie. Opening the print dust, he dips the tip of his brush inside. Knocks off the excess, then twirls the brush lightly between his fingers over the surface of the cracked screen.

"Almost fifty acres."

He exhales a low whistle. "That must be worth a pretty penny. Think that whoever snatched your boyfriend might be interested in a ransom?"

"It's swampland, Agent Richards," I say. And while there *is* a reason why this property would be worth more than most land in Gator Glade, I don't want him to waste time looking in the wrong direction. That's not what this is about. "If they were going to ask for a ransom, they probably would have tried to take me again. Jake has a lot more in assets than I do."

He gives me a tense look. There's something unreadable in his expression. I feel his eyes boring into me. Studying me.

"Tell me about the truck," he says. "The one that had the VIN removed. Where is it?"

"It's at the scrapyard in Gator Glade."

He pauses what he's doing, giving me his full attention as he asks, "What's it doing there?"

I shrug. "You'd have to ask the local sheriff. But the man who runs the place, Jethro Keene, was a friend of my grandfather's. He moved it to one of his bays to keep it safe for me."

He checks his watch. "Then that's where I'll head once I'm finished here. Think this Mr. Keene will give me any trouble?"

I watch as he lifts the three full prints I saw as well as several partials, sticking the tape to the white backing cards. Flipping the device over, he starts the process anew.

"I don't see why he would. But I'll go with you, just in case."

His hand stills. I peer at the phone, thinking he's found something, but if he has, I can't see what.

"That won't be necessary," Agent Richards finally says. He lifts a series of partial prints from the back of Jake's phone and sticks them to a card. Slips the phone back into the bag, seals it, then stands.

"I don't mind."

"But I do."

I stare at him, sure I must have heard wrong.

"That the pheno swab you used?" he asks, pointing to my front pocket.

Glancing down, I nod. When I look back up, he's holding out his hand. After I give it to him, he sets it in his field kit, along with the prints and the phone, and closes the evidence inside.

"You need me, call me. I'll be in touch later."

I follow him to the door, confused, wondering what just happened. It isn't until he marches outside without a backward glance or another word that I figure it out—he thinks that I might have had something to do with Jake's disappearance. I'm a suspect.

CHAPTER 27

Each breath is like a knife to my heart. It feels like my blood is draining from me, pooling in a puddle at my feet. I consider what it would be like to join it. To collapse into a ball and weep. To give up.

But I can't do that.

Because if Agent Richards thinks that I'm involved in what happened, then instead of trying to chase down whoever actually took Jake, he's going to be wasting time figuring out it wasn't me. The help I thought I had has vanished.

I'm on my own.

It's a staggering realization. This is more than I can handle alone. But I don't think I have a choice. I have to do something. I'll never forgive myself if I don't. Terrified or not, I have to figure out how to get Jake back.

Sagging onto the couch, I stare down at my phone, trying to think of my next move. I never put a fan on the casts of the shoe impressions. Between the humidity and the morning dew, there's no way they're dry yet. Agent Richards took Jake's cell with him.

What else is there?

I'm still looking at my screen when it briefly lights, flashing with a text from Director Jacobson—facial recognition has confirmed that Jane Doe is Janine Walker.

The air whooshes out of me, leaving me feeling empty. Deflated. I'd known, and yet I'd hoped… I don't know what, exactly.

My phone lights again, this time as an email she sent comes through. Hopping to my feet, I track down my laptop, finding it still in Butch's bedroom. Bringing it out to the couch, I settle with it on my lap. Wake it from its sleep. A wall of dizziness descends around me, wrapping my head in a thick blanket-like fog as I click to download the attachment Director Jacobson just sent—the case file for my parents' murder.

My heart wrenches, feeling like it's clenched inside an angry fist as I open it. My breathing grows shallow and erratic, a bubble of bile climbing up my throat, threatening to burst as I read the report. Though it lacks the details to make me truly sick, I know what's coming.

Thirty-three years ago, forensics was an entirely different field than it is today. Though the state police had done a thorough job, simply reading about the trace fibers, fingerprints, and blood they collected from the scene is a useless endeavor. Since none of it has turned up any suspects over the years, the evidence would have to be re-examined to be helpful.

While that would no doubt be useful, I don't have time for that. Jake doesn't have time for that.

Assuming that my parents' murders are somehow connected to Janine's disappearance back then—and her reappearance now—I need to figure out what the crime scene can tell me about who I'm dealing with.

Which means looking at the photos.

Though it's been weeks since my last panic attack, the feeling as one wraps itself around me at the mere idea of looking at images of my mom and dad, dead, is all too familiar. A surge of heat rushes to my head. Sweat slicks my skin. My lungs feel like two balloons with a semi parked on top of them.

It doesn't matter how many thousands of similar photographs I've looked at before. These are the people who gave me life. Seeing my family's brutalized bodies is the stuff of nightmares.

But it can't be avoided. Right now, it's all I have to work with.

Besides. This is what I do. And there's no use in being modest—I excel at it.

Like Butch raising me with the skills I'd need to survive dangerous situations as if he knew I'd need them one day, this, too, feels like it was in some way planned. Almost like a part of me somehow anticipated this moment was coming.

If I can do this, I can do anything, including getting Jake back.

My entire body trembles as I scroll down past the written report. As the top edge of the first picture comes into view, I pause a moment as my vision tunnels. Though I don't try to fight against the panic attack, am, in fact, embracing it, using it to sharpen my senses, I need my eyes to work.

I focus on the colors I can see. Slowly, the colors separate into shapes. The shapes into objects. I draw the deepest breath I can. And then I scroll lower.

Image after image tells the same story. The scene is chaotic. Furniture has been overturned. Drawers emptied. Cushions slashed. Knickknacks, mirrors, and glassware broken, shards littering every surface.

The entire house had been ransacked. Even my bedroom had been torn apart, toys and clothes tossed into piles like snowdrifts, the mattress sagging against a wall, the bedframe smashed to pieces.

Someone had been looking for something. And it appears that they'd been desperate to find it.

My first impression is that the killer was disorganized. Frenzied. Angry.

And yet, at the same time, they weren't.

Somehow, they'd managed to subdue both of my parents. Noticing blood in photographs taken in two rooms other than the one my parents died in, I scroll back up to the report.

Serology had matched the drops found in the kitchen to my mom's blood type. The trail that led from the bedroom matched my dad's. Yet somehow, they'd both ended up in the living room, tied to chairs dragged from the dining set. Beaten. Then stabbed repeatedly.

The investigating detectives theorized that it was a home invasion gone wrong, but that's not what I see at all. For one, a knife was used. Stabbing someone is considered an intimate crime. Though it's not an absolute, the use of a knife to murder someone indicates a significant chance that the killer knew their victim.

This was personal.

Two, despite being bound and defenseless, the violence inflicted upon them was complete overkill. Their chairs were also angled so they could watch what was happening to the other, a callous act of cruelty.

This was perverse.

Three, and perhaps the most telling, casts taken from the stab wounds excluded the knife used to perpetrate the crime from matching those found at the house. Every piece from the set my parents owned was accounted for, though the one used to murder my parents had not been left at the scene. The killer had brought the weapon with them.

This was planned.

Though my mom's face is blessedly blurry in each picture, I'm forced to bear witness to the brutality my dad bore with crystal clarity. Each time I force myself to examine the photographs again, making sure there's nothing I missed, it's a shock.

When I'm done, I read the autopsy reports, familiarizing myself with every injury. The depth of the wounds. The muscles, tendons, ligaments, organs, even bones, severed. The force needed to inflict the degree of damage.

Then I close the file. Shut down my computer. And race to the bathroom.

Dropping to the floor, wave after wave of sickness erupts from me. But no matter how much I purge, I can't erase what I've seen. Nor what it could mean.

Because whoever killed my parents knew them. Planned to kill them. Was very angry. And very strong.

Given that after they'd done what they did, Janine Walker left town, never to be heard from again until now, there's one possible culprit who comes to mind. Someone who I know for a fact is both angry and abusive. Dylan Walker. Is it possible that Jake's dad murdered my parents?

CHAPTER 28

I'm not known for my wise decisions. I remind myself of the last time I went knocking on the door of a man I suspected of a crime. Turns out, I was right. He was the serial killer I was after.

He also sprayed me with halothane, an anesthetic used to put patients under before surgery, while I was still on his front doorstep. When I woke up, I was handcuffed to a pole in his basement with a brand on my back.

So yeah. Making a house call by myself is perhaps not the smartest thing I've ever done. But I don't let that stop me from doing it again. Getting out of my car, I march up to the mobile home parked on a very secluded square of land, climb up the steps, and knock on the door.

I find myself taking an involuntary step back as I stare at Dylan Walker a moment later. The man is every bit as tall as Jake, well over six feet. Just as broad. And though he's starting to go soft around his middle as he approaches his sixties, his muscles are still solid.

But what knocks me breathless is his resemblance to his son. It's easy to understand what attracted Janine to him. The strong jaw, the full lips, the perfect Roman nose. What you can't see is the rage responsible for the scars still visible on Jake's flesh—not to mention his psyche—today.

Men like this should come with a warning label,

because looking at him, there's nothing that reveals the monster that lurks beneath. And that's about the only thing I'm sure of right now. Whether he killed my parents or not, the man standing before me *is* a monster.

While I've been studying him, I've felt him doing the same to me. Only, instead of sizing up an opponent, when I take in his expression, Dylan Walker looks like he's seen a ghost.

His voice trembles as he says, "You're Ronnie and Simon's little girl, aren't you?"

It makes me uneasy that he knows who I am. Has he been keeping tabs on me somehow? Waiting for this moment, for their child to show up and confront him about her parents' deaths?

"Why would you say that?" I ask.

"Because it's true, isn't it?" He shakes his head as if to clear the cobwebs from his brain. His gaze looks a little sharper afterward. "It is. I'd recognize you anywhere. They were my best friends, and you? You're an exact mix of them."

He reaches toward me, like he's going to touch my face. My hand moves for the gun holstered at the small of my back. But he seems to realize his mistake before things have a chance to escalate. His arm drops back to his side.

"I'm sorry. I just… You look so much like them." His eyes flit across my face like he's trying to memorize it. My skin crawls, tightening under his examination. Finally, taking a step back from the door, he says, "You should come inside."

Chalking it up as just one more in a series of dumb moves, I step over the threshold into the darkened trailer. Wait as he closes the door, then follow along as he leads the way into the kitchen.

"You want a drink?" he asks, gesturing to an

uncapped bottle of whiskey on the table.

I glance at the vintage Budweiser clock mounted on the wall behind him, Clydesdales trapped behind dingy glass. It isn't even noon yet. But it's already been a long day. One won't kill me. But only one.

"Sure."

I watch closely as he grabs a clean glass from a cabinet and pours a finger of amber liquid into it. Wait until he makes his own drink and takes a sip before knocking mine back, setting the empty tumbler on the table.

Though we both stay standing, neither of us comfortable enough to take a seat, he gives me a grin. "The way you did that? That was just like Simon. Man, I wish he'd been here to see it. He'd have been so proud."

I arch my eyebrows at him. "Proud because I'm an accomplished drinker?"

He points at me, still smiling, then refills both our glasses. "And that right there was pure Ronnie. Your mom never hesitated to call someone out. Wouldn't let anyone get away with anything. Never backed down."

"I bet that pissed you off, didn't it?"

His smile vanishes. "No. That was one of the things I loved about her. She was the bravest woman I've ever met. For that matter, she was braver than any man I've ever met."

"You loved her?" I ask, wondering if it was motive for the crime I suspect he may have committed.

"I loved them both. Growing up, it was just the three of us, running around, raising hell in the swamp. Your mom was such a spitfire, she kept us on our toes. And always laughing."

"My mom was funny?"

Though I know I shouldn't let myself become distracted, I can't help it. I didn't know any of this. The chance to learn more about my parents is intoxicating, making the risk seem worth taking.

"She had the best sense of humor of anyone I've ever known. I mean, just look at your name."

"What about it?"

"Everyone called your grandfather Butch. She named you Cassidy." When I just stare at him, not getting his point, he says, "Come on. Don't tell me your generation has never heard of Butch Cassidy before?"

I haven't, but I imagine myself googling the name sometime next week, when Jake is back, safe and sound, and my parents' murderer has been dealt with. Until then, I need to do my best to keep this interrogation on track.

"What about Janine?"

"She wasn't very funny. But she did love to laugh."

"No, I mean, was she part of your group growing up?"

"Janine didn't move here until later. Eighth grade. But right from the start, she and your mom were close. Half the time, when I think back, I wonder if she and I only got together so we'd fit in better with your parents. They were already a couple by then."

"Did it upset you that she and my dad ended up together?"

"Nah. I always knew it would happen. I knew it even before they did. They were a lot like you and my boy Jake were when you were little. Right from the start, you two were inseparable. It was like Jake thought your mom had given birth to you just for him."

My heart twists inside my chest. It feels like it's been hollowed out with a spoon. For so many years the bond between me and Jake had lived on only in my memory. How many times had I wondered if it was real, or if I had just imagined it?

Then, after being reunited and finding out it was

146

true… how could I have even considered giving that up, for any reason? The whole keeping him safe thing no longer feels noble. It feels cowardly, just one more vulnerability I was too chicken to face.

Now, he's been taken away. Though I've already vowed to do anything it takes to get him back, I make myself another promise—once he's in my arms again, I'm never going to let him go.

Dylan Walker clears his throat. I look up in time to catch him swallowing hard, his face reddened. Turning away, he looks out the window as he wipes his eyes. "He was a good kid. I was hard on him. Too hard. He didn't deserve it. That's my biggest regret in life. Even more than not being there to help your parents when they needed it."

"What would you have done to help them?" I can't resist asking.

Turning back toward me, his eyes still watery, he shrugs. "I don't know. And I can't say if it would have worked, or if I would have ended up like they did. But I still would have liked the chance to try."

"What can you tell me about what happened to them?" His mouth opens and closes like a fish gasping for air as he struggles for words. "I know they were murdered," I add.

He releases a breath, looking relieved, and I wonder how deep Butch's coverup went. If every adult in Gator Glade had been forbidden to tell me the truth.

"Do you know who did it?" I ask. I sharpen my gaze on his face, looking for shame, regret, or even satisfaction. Instead, all I see is grief.

"If I did, I can guarantee you they wouldn't still be walking the Earth today."

"Do you have any theories?"

He shakes his head. "The only thing I could think of

at the time was that maybe Ronnie had stepped on the wrong toes. Like I said, she wasn't scared of anyone. Wouldn't have hesitated to intervene if she saw something bad going down."

I feel a small flare of pride at learning my mom was such a formidable woman. At the same time, it makes me feel worse for being so weak in comparison.

"Heck, she's the one who gave me this, not that I didn't deserve it."

Dylan points to the scar that splits his right eyebrow. "She caught me spanking Jake one day. I'll admit, maybe spanking is too nice of a word for it. Either way, your mom went off on me. Told me not to ever put my hands on him like that again."

His voice cracks as he adds, "I wish I'd listened. I was raised rough. Had always promised myself that if I had kids, I wouldn't treat them the same as I was. I just hadn't expected to face that challenge so young."

He looks at me as if begging me to believe him.

"Me and Janine were only sixteen when she got pregnant. She had Jake our junior year. While my friends were trying to figure out how to scrape up the cash to buy a corsage for their dates to wear to prom, I was working every odd job I could get trying to buy diapers."

Though I promised myself I'd stop at one drink, I take a sip of my refill to keep from interrupting.

"I'm not going to lie and say I didn't resent it. Me and Janine both. Man, the fights we used to get into. She was like your mom, could give it back just as hard as she got it, not that that's any excuse. But after she left, there was no one here to take it but Jake. Do you know that he offered to buy me a house?"

"No, I didn't."

"It's true. When I said I didn't want one, he paid this place off for me instead. I didn't even ask. Thing is, he'll give me any money I need, buy me whatever I want. He just won't be in the same room with me to have a conversation."

His eyes drop to his feet.

"Now that I'm getting older, I realize all my mistakes, see them for what they were. And I'm willing to admit to them. To apologize. I know I don't deserve it, but more than anything I'd like the chance to try to repair my relationship with my boy. Who am I kidding? We don't even have a relationship. We'd have to start from scratch. Still, I'd like to try."

I bite my tongue. I need to get out of here before I say something I might regret.

"I should get going," I mumble.

Dylan nods. "I'm sorry I'm not more help."

He follows me as I leave the kitchen, making my way to the door. I'm reaching for the knob when a new question pops into my mind.

"There is one thing that you might know," I say. "Whose idea was it for me to stay with you that night?"

"Not your mom's, I can tell you that. I'd already started drinking heavily by then. Neither she nor Simon wanted me around you anymore."

"So you think Janine talked them into it?"

"She must have. I have no idea what she said. I imagine she must have promised not to take her eyes off you or leave you alone with me, something of the sort, but if that's what happened, she lied."

"What do you mean?"

"She came in carrying you. Put you to sleep in Jake's room, then left. Didn't come back until morning, and when she did, she took you. That was the last I ever saw her."

"Do you know where she took me?"

He nods. "I was told she went to your parents' house.

That when they didn't answer, she took you to Butch's. Your grandfather told her to stay at his place with you while he went to check on them."

"Butch is the one who found my parents?"

"He was. I'm not sure how long it took him after he called the cops to get back home to you, but when he did, Janine left. That's the last anyone ever saw of her."

"Any idea why?"

"At first, I thought she was just grieving. Some people have weird ways of doing that, you know. I figured she'd be back after she calmed down a bit. But when she never came home, well, I knew that whoever had killed your parents must have got her, too."

I give him a close look, wondering if he really believes that, or if he somehow knows she's still alive. Mistrust ripples beneath my skin as I tear my eyes from his and make a hasty escape.

"You're welcome back any time. No need to be a stranger," he says to my back as I walk through the door.

I turn and give him a tight smile.

"And if you ever run into my son… could you maybe tell him to give me a chance? He'll listen to—. You know what? Never mind about that. But whether you talk to him about me or not, now that you're back in town, look him up, will you?"

"Why?" I ask, curiosity getting the better of me.

"Because he deserves to be happy."

"What makes you think he's not?"

He shrugs. "Even if he is, he'd be even happier with you in his life. Trust me. Like I said, you and Jake are like Ronnie and Simon were—meant to be together. Give it a chance and see if I'm not right."

I hurry back to my car before I can change my mind. Before I do something silly like give Dylan Walker a hug. Because somehow, he knew what I needed to hear.

Some parents have a knack for that. The problem is, some sociopaths do, too.

CHAPTER 29

My thoughts race as I drive home, unsure what to believe. Dylan Walker had seemed genuinely upset when he talked about what happened to my parents. But was it real? Or did he simply put on a good show? I can't decide.

True, he said he thought that Janine had been gone all these years because she'd been killed by the same person who murdered my parents, but he could have done that to purposely throw me off. He could know she's still alive.

More than that. He could have known exactly where she was this whole time. Could have even been keeping her locked up somewhere.

It's possible, especially out here in the swamp. With houses so far away from each other, he wouldn't even have to worry about anyone hearing her.

And then, after she somehow managed to escape, he could have had Jake kidnapped to use as bait to get her back. Or as leverage to keep her quiet. He told me that Jake gave him whatever money he wanted. He could have used some of it to pay someone to take his son.

Maybe that's even how the man in the fancy shoes makes his living—by snatching people. But none of that explains why he broke into my house before Janine crashed her car. Or why he tried to take me from the parking garage.

I know I'm reaching, grabbing at straws. I'm so desperate to have a direction to focus my efforts in that I'm at risk of losing my way entirely. I can't let that happen.

Growling in frustration, I turn into the sanctuary driveway. Groan as I see the SUV parked in front of me, blocking the way. Getting out of my car, I keep my head held high as I approach Agent Richards.

"Back so soon?" I ask, brushing past him to run my fingers lightly over the top of one of the casts. They come away slightly tacky. It's still too soon to remove them. That's probably the only reason why they, and Agent Richards, are still here.

"I was able to lift an image of the VIN on that car. It was a match to the one Agent Chan thought it might be."

I know I should ask what he thinks it means. If crooked cops are somehow involved in all this, or if he has any ideas about how the vehicle disappeared from the impound lot where it was being held and came to be in Janine's possession. But my temper responds for me before I can get it under control.

"Have you figured out a way for me to be responsible for that yet, despite being in Virginia when it was stolen? Or are you still working on that?"

He gives me a look that lets me know he thinks I'm being difficult. I give him one back that lets him know that I think he's a jerk.

When he doesn't respond, I turn on my heel and head toward the house. I hear him following behind me, not a smart move on his part.

"Listen, how well do you know your boyfriend?"

"Well enough."

"Are you sure about that?"

"What do you mean?" I ask, glancing at him over

my shoulder.

"I might as well get this out of the way. I had a colleague look him up for me. He found some things that suggest your boyfriend might not exactly be on the up-and-up."

I come to a halt so suddenly he almost runs into me. He wheels back as I spin to face him.

"What are you talking about?" I demand.

"Well, to start, he supposedly donates over seventy percent of his income, but when you start digging into the details, they're pretty shady. We're talking layers upon layers concealing where the money actually goes. Why would that be necessary if it's the truth? Where's it all going?"

I motion toward the land around us. "Right here. To the sanctuary."

"Here?"

"Yes."

"Then why the coverup?"

Continuing toward the house, I say, "Because he didn't want my grandfather to know where the money was coming from. That he was the one keeping this place afloat."

"But why? That makes no sense. I mean, if I was shacking up with some guy's granddaughter—"

Pausing on the doorstep, I give him a sharp look. "Shacking up?"

He returns it with one of his own as I open the door and step inside. Though I debate not letting him in the house, turning him away and telling him to leave, my curiosity to see where he's going with this wins and I allow him entrance.

"Listen. We both know that part of the job is looking for the things that people don't want to see on their own. So, yeah. When I was in here alone earlier, after I first arrived, I took a peek around. And I couldn't help but notice a bag of his clothes back there in the room—the *only* room—with a bed in it."

"What's your point?"

"My point is that you might not be seeing the situation clearly. I had someone look into you, too. I know what happened to you, what you've been through. And I know that you've been down here what, three weeks, and this guy's already moved in?"

Before I can argue he holds his hands up.

"Listen, I'm not trying to judge you. But we both know that you're vulnerable right now. So you need to keep an open mind and hear me out. Can you really say that it's absolutely impossible that this guy left on his own accord?"

"His truck is still here. He left his keys. We're in the middle of nowhere. Where do you think he went?"

"I don't know. It's possible that he called someone to pick him up."

"If you believe that, subpoena his phone records and check."

"I'm already on it." He sighs heavily, something like pity on his face. "I'm not trying to be cruel here. Honestly. But what actual proof do you have that he was taken?"

I grapple for an answer, because the truth is, I don't have proof. The part of the driveway where I found Jake's phone isn't covered by any of the surveillance cameras. Even when the casts dry, if one's a match for the overpriced shoes worn by the man who attacked me at the hospital, that still doesn't prove that he took Jake by force.

I know what Agent Richards is trying to do. I've done the same thing myself while working a case. But the truth is, most of the time there isn't indisputable proof in a situation like this. He knows that as well as I do. If he wants to play Devil's advocate, fine, but he better be quick about it because Jake needs our help. We don't have time to waste.

"Does this mean that you no longer think I'm a suspect?"

"No. That's still a possibility."

Rolling my eyes, I mutter, "Ridiculous."

"Possible, but not likely. And you know you shouldn't be upset by that because if our situations were reversed, you'd think the same thing. Admit it."

Though I probably would, I don't concede. "So why are you here? What is it that you're hoping to accomplish?"

"I'm looking for answers, same as you. But all I keep coming up with is more questions."

"Join the club."

"You say that someone broke into your house looking for something?"

"I didn't know they were looking for anything at first. Not until they tried to snatch me from the parking garage."

"Was Jake staying here before the break-in?"

"No."

"So how do you know that he wasn't here so he could look for whatever the other guy failed to find?"

"Because Jake's had free rein over this house for years. Decades, even. Anything he wanted, my grandfather or I would have let him have."

"It's easy to say that when you don't know what it is that's wanted."

"Agent Richards, Jake got shot protecting me from the person who murdered my grandfather. I told him to run, and he chose to stay and throw himself in front of the gun instead. If your line of questioning were true, wouldn't it have been easier—and certainly less risky—for him to just let me be killed and then come back and search the place?"

"You have a point. But that doesn't prove he didn't take off on his own for another reason."

"Like what?"

"Help me understand the dynamics we're dealing with here. Tell me how the two of you got together. What your relationship is like."

Snatching the photograph from the top of Butch's keepsake box, I hold it out for Agent Richards to see.

"This is us."

"You're the baby?"

"Yes."

"Your head was huge."

"True, but that's not the point. You wanted to know about our relationship. Well, here it is."

"Are you trying to say that you guys have always been an item?"

"No. But I think it was always in our future. I've measured every man I've ever dated against Jake. And not one of them even stood a chance."

Agent Richards sets his palm gently on my wrist. Pushes the hand holding the picture down from between us. "But how do you know he feels the same?" He takes a step closer to me. "Don't get me wrong, he'd have to be an idiot not to, but the world is full of idiots."

He releases my arm and takes me by the shoulders. I swallow hard as he stares into my eyes with an intensity that makes it impossible for me to look away.

"What I'm trying to say here is, you at least need to consider that you coming down here, this whole instant family thing, maybe it was too much too soon for him. Maybe he panicked, and with everything that's been going on, he saw an out and decided to take it."

The expression on his face tells me that this is the theory he believes. That Jake chose to leave. Even if that meant feeding me to the wolves.

CHAPTER 30

I can't believe it. I won't. Even if I can't prove otherwise. Even though it makes a sick sort of sense. After all, how many stories are there about men who went to the store to grab something, only to run out on their families?

And Jake and I aren't even really a family. I run what's happened since I came back to Gator Glade through my mind, looking for clues that what Agent Richards is suggesting is possible. Have I been too needy? Too damaged? Did he take off because he's upset I tried to push him away to keep him safe?

Maybe we have moved too fast. It's possible he'd been as lonely as I was. Now that his mom's back in the picture, maybe that's no longer the case.

But even if all that is true, I know Jake. Deep down in my soul know him. And I know he never would have left like that.

He's a good man. Kind. If things were moving too fast or he decided he didn't want to be with me, he'd have the guts to tell me. He wouldn't just disappear because it was easier.

Even if Janine came here looking for him and he decided to go with her, he would have said something. Even if she tried to talk him out of it and told him it was too dangerous, he still would have found a way to get word to me, if only to keep me away from the risk of searching for him.

I have to figure out who took him and what they want so I can get him back. But I'm not sure I can do that alone. Even if I can, it will definitely be easier with help. Which means that, for at least the time being, I have to find a way to play nice and keep Agent Richards on my side.

"I'm not trying to upset you," he says, tightening his grip on my shoulders.

"I know." I turn, breaking his grasp on me, and set the photograph back in Butch's box.

"But you can't stick your head in the sand. There's a reason why serial killers' wives always claim that they never suspected a thing. It's because they didn't want to. But you're smarter than that, Agent Knox. You need to be realistic about what's really going on here."

My mouth drops. Did he really just compare me to a woman who doesn't know that her husband's hobby is killing people?

"Now, I'd like for you to fill me in on some more of the details about what's going on here so I can get a better grasp on what I'm dealing with."

I need a breather before I do something I regret. Forcing a smile, I say, "Why don't we hold off on that. It's been a long day—for both of us. I imagine you must be ready for some sleep."

"Actually, I'd prefer to power through and discuss it now, if you don't mind."

I resist the urge to groan, nodding instead before I walk into the kitchen to make some coffee. A wave of exhaustion crashes against me as I put fresh grounds in the basket.

Agent Richards' steps approach behind me. "When your director first contacted me, it was because of the woman who went missing."

I nod.

"And this woman? She never told anyone who she was before she left the hospital?"

"No, but… Director Jacobson confirmed her ID this morning using facial recognition. It was Jake's mother."

Agent Richards looks at me like I've grown a second head. "What? Why am I just hearing about this now?"

"Because I only found out after you left this morning. We weren't sure—we couldn't be. She left over thirty years ago. Neither Jake nor I have seen her since then."

"When did you realize it could be her? I mean, in relation to when Jake went missing?"

"Not long. Not even an hour."

"Un-freaking-believable."

"Excuse me?"

"Listen, I feel bad for what you've been through. I do. But we all know the risks when we sign on for a job like this."

"What are you talking about?"

"I'm talking about how you need to get help."

"That's why you're here, isn't it?" I ask. "To help?"

"I'm here to determine if there's an actual case or not. And that's just what I've done. There's not."

"But—"

"Doesn't it strike you as odd that I'm here on my own?"

"When Director Jacobson first called, it was for someone to conduct a magneto-optical imaging analysis on the missing VIN of the truck that crashed. I doubt that takes more than one person."

"But when she called again, it was for your missing boyfriend."

I shrug. "I figured you were all they could spare."

"When she spoke with me, her only concern was for the fastest response possible. She must have known that you were unraveling. That this was all just a big waste of time. It's just too bad that time was mine, because the kind of help you need is beyond my abilities."

"Get out," I say, barely above a whisper.

"Don't they have you seeing a therapist or something?"

"Get out!"

This time it's a yell. I don't need him. The truth is, I don't need anyone. I never have, not really. Butch raised me to be that way.

It's the fear I've felt since I woke up in that basement that made me forget that. But now I'm starting to remember.

Brushing past Agent Richards, I cross the living room, yank the door wide, and point at the opening. The second he's through I slam it behind him and lock it. Stand there watching out the window until he disappears from view. Then I make myself count to a hundred.

Once I'm sure he's gone, I let myself lose it, roaring in frustration. Push over a box of painting supplies as I storm across the living room. Kick the corner of the couch on my way by.

I knew that my time with the FBI was almost over. This shouldn't be such a shock. But it is. I'm completely on my own, with no one to turn to. It's enough to make me admit defeat.

Only, that will never happen. Even when I was handcuffed to a metal support pole in a serial killer's basement, I didn't do that. Or when I lost the only family member I had left in this world. I'm not a quitter.

Jake is out there somewhere, in need of help, despite what everyone else might think. If I can't pull myself together and figure this out, my career might not be the only casualty. I'll never forgive myself if I let that happen.

I rub my chest, but it doesn't make my heart ache any less. On my own or not, I have to believe that I can do this. I just need to vent my anger so I can think clearly. I need to rip something to shreds.

I hesitate only a second in the doorway to Butch's room before stomping inside. Grabbing a fistful of carpet from the far corner, I give it a tug. Grunt as I struggle to pull it loose, stumbling backward when it finally gives.

Moving down a step, I curl my fingers around the edge, draw a deep breath, and release a primal howl as I yank. This time, the flooring pulls free much easier, my momentum sending me halfway across the room, where I land in a heap.

Hot tears fill my eyes, but I refuse to give in. Swallowing down the urge to cry, I crawl forward, to where the carpet has flopped back down into place. Already I can feel my rage abating. A grim smile torques my lips as I curl my fingers around the end of the rug, preparing to destroy it.

But something sharp brushes against my hand, making me pause. I lean forward to take a look. Frown in confusion.

I pin the edge of the carpet under my knee and stare down at the large plastic freezer bag that had been hiding beneath it. There appear to be Polaroid pictures inside it, but it's too dim to see what's on them. And when I pick up the bag for a closer look, it's clear by the weight that it contains something more.

Standing, I carry the bag into the en suite bathroom and flick on the light. Feel my throat snap shut. But it's not the photographs that have caused the reaction—it's what's in the Ziploc with them.

I glance over my shoulder at the spot I'd found the

package, tucked right under the edge of the rug, on top of the carpet pad. There's no way it got there by accident, which means someone must have hidden it. But who? Butch?

Since it was his room, that seems the most likely answer, but what would he be doing with a bloody knife? And, given the obvious answer to that question, why would he have kept it when it would be so much easier—and smarter—to get rid of it?

I shuffle the contents inside, hoping for a better clue. And find myself looking at a pair of familiar faces that suck the last of the air from my lungs. Faces that I haven't seen in person since I was five years old. I raise the bag closer to my face, not believing my eyes. But it's true.

Even though I've already suffered the shock of seeing my parents' bodies today, this time, it's worse. Because in these pictures, they're not dead. They're still very much alive. The terror on both of their faces makes that clear.

With a sudden, sickening sensation, I realize that the knife inside the bag that I hold must be the one that was used to kill them. I drop the package instinctively, backing away with my hands held up.

There's no way that Butch was the one to hide this baggie. He never would have concealed evidence like this. Because the photographs don't just show my parents, but the knife clenched in the fist of a man with a horned mermaid tattooed on his bicep. The man who murdered them.

This must have been what the people who broke in were looking for. And I know who told them it was here. The same person who must have hidden it, in the last place the killer would think to look, before she left town. Janine Walker.

CHAPTER 31

It doesn't make sense. Jake's mom knew who was responsible for my parents' deaths, yet she never told anyone. Worse than that—she had evidence. And instead of turning it over to the authorities so they could bring the killer to justice, it's been hiding under the edge of the carpet in my grandfather's bedroom for the last thirty-three years.

The baggie on the floor in front of me must be why she was on her way here the day she crashed—to collect it. Which means that whoever stopped her is likely also the person who has Jake.

But is that person Dylan Walker? Or someone else?

Scooping up the package, I hold it up to the light, taking a closer look at the killer's tattoo. The horned mermaid is inked in vibrant shades of blue and green and purple.

The artist was incredibly skilled, creating a piece that's intricate and detailed. This isn't the kind of ink that gets done in prison, or even at any of the run-of-the-mill shops tucked into strip malls across the country.

Bottom line—it wasn't cheap.

Could Dylan Walker have afforded something like this over three decades ago? Though it doesn't seem likely, I close my eyes and imagine myself back in his kitchen. Try to visualize his arms, the length of his sleeves on the shirt he wore.

Even if the ink had been faded by the Florida sun over the years, surely I would have noticed if there'd been unnatural colors on the man's skin. But the truth is, I can't be sure. I'd been preoccupied, on guard.

It's possible the tattoo belongs to Jake's dad. It's just as possible it doesn't. But there's one person who knows for sure.

I jump to my feet, heart racing. I have to find Janine. But first, I have to make sure no one else can find the baggie. It's the only leverage I have. Where should I hide it?

The toilet tank? Too obvious. My gaze lifts to the ceiling. The exhaust fan? No. Anyone used to conducting searches would check there. I consider the rest of the house, the outbuildings, the barn, when I catch my own eyes in the bathroom mirror. But it's not my exhausted reflection that draws me closer.

My phone rings, the sound amplified by the tiny space. I pull it from my pocket on autopilot. Frown when I see the name on the screen.

I reject the call. I don't need to speak with Director Jacobson right now. The only person I need to talk to is Janine Walker.

Setting the plastic bag down, I bring up the camera app on my cell, zooming in to take a shot of the tattoo. Then, pocketing the device, I curl my fingers along the edge of the mirror and pull.

The phone vibrates with another incoming call as the medicine cabinet door swings open. Removing the half-empty bottle of aspirin and a full sleeve of razor cartridges from the shelf inside, I grab on and start jiggling.

Nothing happens at first, but then, slowly, it starts to give. I continue working until I have the cabinet out of the wall. Placing it carefully on the floor, I lift myself onto the counter and peer inside the hole left behind.

There's a cross brace between the two studs the cabinet was set between about eighteen inches down. I stick my arm in the opening, making sure I can reach the wood. I can. It's perfect.

Hopping down, I grab the package and lower it through the hole. Then I work the medicine cabinet back in place, return the items inside, and clean up the drywall dust.

When I'm finished, I stand back and inspect my work until I'm confident that I haven't left a trace of what I've done. I change my clothes, pulling on a pair of cargo pants, boots, and a baggy shirt so I can conceal two firearms—one in an ankle holster, the other inside my waistband—just in case. Then I grab my keys and wallet out of my purse and hit the road.

The entire drive to the hospital, I plan.

When Janine first went missing, back when her identity was still unknown, I'd checked the streets immediately surrounding the hospital, looking for surveillance cameras. Originally, it seemed likely that she must have called someone to pick her up.

I no longer suspect that's the case. If she had, I doubt the plastic baggie and its contents would have still been in Butch's room for me to find.

That means she fled on foot. Considering the condition she was in, she couldn't have gone far.

Reaching the hospital, I drive by, spiraling outward. There are a handful of small businesses and doctor's offices. A number of well-maintained homes. Others that could use some love. And then I find it.

That house, the one that's the bane of neighborhoods the world over. Overgrown yard, boarded-up windows, neglect so strong you can smell it. If you search long enough, you'll find it. Janine must have known that as well.

Pulling past, I park along the curb down the street and backtrack, senses on high alert as I approach. From a distance, the door looks solid. But I can see what appears to be a thin trail in the overgrown brush leading around back.

I check my surroundings, making sure that I'm not being watched. Given the width of the narrow path, it's easy to assume that it was made by an animal. But, as I prove to myself as I leave the sidewalk and stay on the already damaged grass, a human can travel through it as well.

A crumbling cement stoop leads to a back door that's been replaced by a sheet of plywood. And though the wood might have once been nailed in place over the opening, now it's simply propped against it.

Slipping my gun from the holster clipped inside the back of my pants, I creep forward, pausing after each step to listen. Crouching, I press my spine against the back of the house and edge closer to the hole. I hear nothing besides the droning buzz of bees and the call of a bird somewhere in the distance.

I ease the wood away, creating a gap just big enough to slip inside, letting it settle back into place immediately once I'm through. Though the interior is almost completely devoid of light, I can see that I'm in a kitchen.

I stay where I am, blinking in the darkness, waiting for my eyes to adjust, the buzzing louder now. Much louder, almost as if the bees are using the house as their hive.

But the slightly sweet odor that permeates the room around me isn't honey. And I realize the buzzing isn't made by bees.

Raising an arm, I press it against my nose. Draw

shallow breaths in through my mouth. Resist the urge to bolt.

Had leaving the hospital too soon been a fatal decision? Had Janine succumbed to her injuries? Or has something else happened here? Because as the shape of the body lying on the floor in front of me slowly separates from the shadows, it becomes clear—someone isn't leaving this house alive.

CHAPTER 32

Sweat beads to the surface of my skin as the heat inside the house quickly grows overwhelming. My skin longs to feel a breeze, my lungs to fill with fresh air. But that can't happen until I've searched the building. And I know it's only going to get worse before it gets better.

The drone of the flies seems louder now that I know what they are—and why they're here. Though I try to keep my gaze off the body on the floor, I can't help looking at the corpse.

The mouth is slack. The eyes milky and glazed. There's a crater where the left side of the skull should be. Judging by the maggots squirming in the wound, this person's been dead at least twenty-four hours.

Whoever's responsible may no longer be here, and yet, I keep my grip tight on the gun, the weapon aimed toward the ceiling. My senses are on full alert as I creep across the kitchen.

I press my back against the wall as I prepare to turn the corner into the next room. Work to steady my breathing. A slow and steady inhale. A controlled exhale. Another breath in, then I pivot into the living room, ready to lower the gun, to aim, to fire if need be.

No one is there.

I search the shadows, making sure I'm alone. I am. But the half-eaten can of beans abandoned in the middle of the empty floor, not yet swarmed by insects, suggests that someone was just here.

The lock on the front door is still latched. All the windows are boarded. The only way out is behind me. Which means that whoever it is, they're still here.

My heart hammers as I stalk down the hall toward two opposing open doorways. The killer is in one of the rooms. But I can't check them both at once, which means I'll be forced to turn my back to one of them, leaving me vulnerable to attack. It's an impossible choice—but one I have to make.

The heat in the unconditioned house is stifling, making it hard to think. My eyes sting from the salt in my sweat. My brain feels like it's boiling.

Instinctively, when given the choice, most people go to their right. Knowing that, if it were me, I'd choose to shelter in the room on the left. But what the rooms are also factors into the decision. Not knowing if one is a bathroom versus a bedroom puts me at further disadvantage.

But I have to choose, and soon, because all delaying is going to do is give me time to overthink this and psych myself out. I'm going left.

There's no relief at having made a decision—because the wrong one could prove fatal. It makes me long to go outside, to guard the door and call the police, let them deal with this. But if I do that, I won't be the one to question the person inside.

And it has to be me.

So I push on. Do my best to keep my nerves in check as I prepare to enter the room on my left. My pulse thunders so loud in my ears that I almost don't hear the soft rustle of fabric coming from the room on my right. I turn at the last moment, leveling the gun at the figure rushing toward me.

"Janine, stop! It's me! Cassidy!"

The woman draws to a sudden halt. I tuck my gun back into the holster as she stares at me with widened eyes, nostrils flaring, the chunk of concrete in her fist, no doubt from the crumbling doorstep out back, stained by the blood of the man lying dead on the kitchen floor. The one wearing a pair of fancy, ridiculously expensive shoes.

"Cassidy?" A bit of the ferocity in her expression eases as she takes me in, studying my face. "Oh, thank God you're here!"

She flings herself at me, throwing her arms around my torso. I'm mindful of the placement of her hand holding the weapon at my back. But I hear it hit the floor as she melts against me.

"Are you okay?" I ask, pulling away enough to see her face. Her huge eyes, her sunken cheeks, the shading of her bruises visible even in the shadows.

She nods, wiping at a tear rolling down her cheek. "I was hoping you'd find me. That's why I stayed here, even after—" her voice breaks off in a whimper.

"I saw," I tell her.

"I didn't have a choice. He was going to kill me."

"Do you know who he is?"

"No. But I know who he worked for."

"Who?" I ask.

But she just shakes her head in response.

"It's okay. You can trust me."

"I know, sweetie. Oh, but aren't you a sight for sore eyes. You look so much like your momma."

A sob escapes her as she tucks a strand of hair behind my ear. I swallow down a lump of emotion. I need some fresh air. And we need to get out of here before anyone else comes.

Taking her by the hand, I give it a squeeze, then lead

her toward the kitchen. She balks as we reach the doorway.

"I don't think I can go in there," she says.

"It's the only way out."

"I know. I just… I never thought I'd be able to do something like that."

"Janine, who did he work for?" I press.

"You're better off not knowing. He's a very dangerous man."

"Whoever he is, he has Jake."

"What?" She ages a decade before my eyes, her entire body dragged down by gravity. She clutches at my arm, her skeletal fingers digging painfully deep. "My Jake?"

"Yes."

"But how? How do they know he's my son?"

"I'm not sure they do. They might have taken him to get to me, not you."

"You and Jake?" she whispers. Her eyes widen as they search my face. "That was him, wasn't it? The man trying to help get me out of the truck after I crashed."

"Yes."

"We have to get him back."

"I intend to. But I don't know who I'm dealing with here, Janine. Or what he wants. But I think that maybe you do."

Her gaze darts away, but not before I see the terror in it.

"I need you to tell me what's going on."

She nods, still not looking at me. "I will. But not here."

"Then let's go."

As I help the limping woman past the body and out of the house as swiftly as possible, I know I should call in the crime scene we're leaving behind. I know, but I don't care. Because if I do, there will be questions. Even an anonymous report might get traced back to me.

The fear in Janine's expression made it clear—I don't have time for that. Not if I want a chance to get Jake back while he's still alive.

CHAPTER 33

I stare at the woman across from me as if I'm trying to drink in everything about her, afraid to miss a thing. The way she looks. The way she moves. The way she studies me from her seat, as if she finds me as fascinating as I find her.

But my mouth grows uncomfortably dry under her scrutiny. Or maybe it's from all the words I keep forcing myself to swallow. Because there are just so many questions I want to ask her. So many answers I know she holds. But I'm afraid to scare her off.

I need her, certainly much more than she needs me. She holds all the power. Sitting here at the table in Butch's kitchen, that's clear now more than ever.

Because it was one thing to avoid conversation in the car on the drive here, when the lull of the road put her to sleep. It's another to continue to stay silent while fully awake, watching me like a specimen under a microscope.

But that's exactly what she does, her hands wrapped around a cup of coffee, though she's yet to take a sip. And it's taking every bit of willpower I have to be patient and not jump across the table to shake the secrets she holds inside of her loose.

This woman was my mom's best friend. I've heard stories about how close they were, how they were inseparable, how they did everything together. But only one of them wound up dead. The other has been missing for over thirty years. I want to know how that happened, and why.

"I can't believe how grown you are," she says, so softly I barely hear her. But it's a relief to have the silence between us finally broken. "And how much you look like Ronnie."

My hands curl tighter around my mug. Though I've heard plenty of people talk about my mom over the years, until today, only Butch ever called her Ronnie. To everyone else, she was Veronica.

But now, it appears that those closest to her used the nickname. First Dylan Walker, and now Janine.

"And Jake." Her voice cracks as she says his name. "I didn't even recognize my own baby."

The sharpness of Janine's gaze relaxes. The result takes me by surprise, leaving me breathless.

Earlier, I'd thought Jake looked like his dad. He has his father's strong jaw, full lips, and perfect nose. But now, I see that he has his mother's eyes.

A rush of recognition sweeps over me, leaving me with the sensation that I know her better than I do. It's disconcerting. Because I don't know her at all.

She wipes at a tear trailing down her cheek and sniffs. "It's been so long. Too long. I've missed everything."

I brace myself for her explanation.

Instead, she says, "You know, your mom and I always dreamed the two of you would end up together. We had your wedding all planned out. Your dress, the flowers, the cake."

It's something I've always wondered—what my mom dreamt of for my future. But as much as a part of me longs to know these details, I realize how unimportant they are. They're part of a future I'll never have. My mom's hopes and dreams for me died over thirty years ago—with her.

And this woman sitting across from me knows why that is. More importantly, she knows who has Jake. Impatience surges under my skin.

Though I try to temper my tone, my words come out harsh as I ask, "Why'd you leave?"

"Oh, sweetie. I had to."

"Because of the dangerous man? The one who sent that guy back at the abandoned house after you?"

"Yes."

"The one who has Jake?"

Looking away, she nods.

"The one who killed my parents."

Her eyes latch onto mine, the sharpness in them back even stronger than before.

"How do you know that?"

"I didn't. Not for sure. But now that you've confirmed it, I'm trying to figure out why you're trying to protect this man instead of telling me who he is."

"Cassidy, I'm trying to protect *you*."

"Don't worry about me."

"Your momma—"

"Is dead," I interrupt. "My dad, too. And now Butch. I have one person left in this world and I'll be damned if I'm just going to sit here doing nothing while I lose him. So cut the crap, Janine. Who is this guy?"

Her expression tightens, gaze hardening to stone. As it does, any resemblance between her and Jake vanishes.

"He's the man your momma stole money from."

The answer hits me in the stomach like a battering ram. I struggle to catch my breath. Seek comfort in the only place it's to be found—that Jake's dad wasn't my parents' killer.

"That's the reason why *I* had to leave. When she didn't tell him where that money was, I didn't want to be next."

She glares at me with pure venom, but I refuse to back down.

"How do you know?" I ask, pushing my coffee to the side as I lean across the table, hands curled into fists.

"How do I know what?"

"That she didn't tell him where the money was? If you weren't there, how do you know?"

"Because I *was* there."

It was a test. One I didn't think she would pass, but she did. Because someone had to take those pictures I found hidden in Butch's room.

"How did you escape?"

"Because he didn't know I was there."

"Why didn't you go to the police? Turn him in?"

"It was too dangerous. Some of them work for him. I didn't know who."

"What's his name?"

"Cassidy."

She reaches out, covering my hand with her own. I jerk it away.

"What. Is. His. Name."

"Nico Castellanos. But trust me, Cassidy. You don't want to mess with this guy. He's too dangerous."

"He has your son."

"But I don't have what he wants."

"Do you know how to contact him?"

Janine looks away, shaking her head as she stares down into her coffee.

"Then I guess I'll just have to give his name to the police and take my chances."

Her eyes dart back to my face. "Please don't do that," she whispers.

"What choice to I have? Unless you know another way?"

"I can get him a message. If you promise not to go to the cops, I'll make a call to someone who can reach him."

"Have them tell him I have what he's looking for."

"Cassidy, he isn't the type of man you bluff. He won't hesitate to—" She swallows hard. Though her voice has grown tenser and higher pitched, it's devoid of emotion as she says, "He won't hesitate to kill you when he finds out that you don't. Or Jake."

"Then I guess I better not let him find out."

"I really wish you'd rethink—"

I push back from the table, standing so suddenly that the chair I was sitting on hits the floor behind me.

"I'm not asking you to do this with me. Just to get him the message. Find out where he wants me to meet him to make the exchange. Tell him he'll get what he wants as long as he brings Jake and he's okay. After you do that, you're free to leave. I'll see that you get wherever it is you want to go."

Pointing to Butch's ancient landline hanging on the wall, I add, "Now, make the call."

Turning to leave, I pick up my chair from the floor and push it under the table, leaving my cell phone on the seat where it can't be seen. Then I storm from the kitchen without a backward glance and head outside, slamming the front door after me.

I'm vibrating as I leave the house, but I know I have to find a way to keep it together, no matter how badly I want to fall apart. So much is depending on me. And any mistake, even a tiny one, could prove fatal.

CHAPTER 34

My breathing is labored. My muscles strain. But the ache feels good. It helps center me. Helps clear my mind and keep me in the present. I need that now more than ever.

Because what's going on here? It's just getting started.

I'm playing a dangerous game with a deadly opponent and I have no choice but to go into battle alone, without backup. The last time I did that, I found myself held captive in a serial killer's basement. But I also found myself the victor.

Are the odds any better in my favor this time? No. If anything, they're worse. The stakes are much higher. I have no idea what I'm heading into. And it's not just my life that's on the line this time.

The labor of mucking out stalls is tedious but welcome. It makes me feel strong. Capable. It keeps me distracted, stops the panic from building under my skin.

So distracted that I don't notice that Janine has come out until I place the pitchfork on top of the manure in the wheelbarrow and push it out of Daisy's stall. I startle as I spot her standing against the far wall, watching me work.

"It's done then?" I ask. "Your contact is going to give Nico the message?"

"It's done."

"How will I know his response?"

"He has his ways. Trust me. When there's something to know, you'll know."

I set my load down, then latch the door behind me. Turn to find her giving me a small, wistful smile.

Leaning against the wall, I watch her curiously. As does Stephano. Sensing my uneasiness, the tiny goat stays by my side.

"You know, I think I spent more time here than at my own house when I was a teenager. Butch was the sweetest man. I was sorry when I saw that he had passed."

It's the first time she's mentioned Butch. I hadn't been aware she knew, but if she saw his obituary, wherever she's been, it can't have been too far away.

"And your mom loved it here. She loved everything about this place."

She sticks her hand in the zebras' stall for them to sniff and clucks to get their attention. Daisy swings her head to look, snorts and goes back to her dinner.

"She'd be proud of you, you know. She was brave, like you. Gutsy. Protected the people she loved like a tiger."

It's similar to what Dylan said about my mom and I can't help feeling a fresh pang of loss, wondering how different my life would have been if she'd been a part of it.

"How did she get wrapped up in this mess?" I ask.

Janine looks away, studying the ground at her feet. "It was an insanely hot summer. We had you kids down by the Ten Thousand Islands area for a paddle when you found something. A package in the water."

"I thought you said she stole money?"

"A kilo of cocaine *is* money," she says. "Big

money."

My mouth drops. I've heard of people finding bricks of drugs off the Keys, but never in the water off the Everglades. That doesn't mean it doesn't happen, though.

"Why didn't you turn it in?" I ask.

"She thought about it. But then she thought about what she could use all that money for."

"She? As in, only her?"

"You found it. She took possession of it."

"And what? Just cut you out of the picture? Decided to become a drug dealer?"

"Yes and yes."

Janine sighs heavily, staring at her hand as she twirls a piece of hay between her fingers.

"What did she need the money for?" I ask.

"To start over."

"What do you mean?"

She looks at me with sad eyes. "I mean, she was unhappy. She hadn't always been, but things at home weren't great."

"You mean with my dad?"

"Yes."

It doesn't make any sense. True, every image of my parents that I hold in my mind was stolen from a photograph. I don't have one memory of either of their faces that doesn't come from a picture. But I remember the way I felt when I was little.

Safe. Loved. Happy.

I remember stirring pancake batter when we all made breakfast together on the weekends. Movie nights snuggled on the couch where I'd pretend to be asleep, trying my best not to giggle when they started kissing. Most of all, I remember laughter.

Had I blocked out memories of the not so good

times?

"It's not always easy spending your entire life in the same tiny town. She knew that if she stayed, that's what would happen."

"But you just said how much she loved this place."

"You can love something and want more at the same time, Cassidy."

"Was she planning on taking me with her?"

Janine shrugs.

"The man who killed her? Nico Castellanos?" I commit the name to memory, vowing to make mine as painful to him as his is to me. Knowing that this won't truly be over until one of us is gone. "How did he find out she was the one who had his drugs?"

"The package had his stamp on it. A mermaid with horns."

The same image as the tattoo on the man in the Polaroids I have hidden inside. The ones Janine doesn't know I've found.

"One of the people your mom took the drugs to when she was trying to sell them recognized the design. It's how dealers mark their property, a warning in case they fall into the wrong hands."

"But if the person who finds it doesn't know—"

Janine shakes her head. "It doesn't matter. That's not how these guys operate. They don't give warnings. They make statements. Teach lessons."

"Did she know he was coming for her?"

"Are you sure about doing this, Cassidy? It's not too late to change your mind."

"Did she?"

"Let's not talk about that, sweetie. It won't accomplish anything. Tell me about you instead. When you're not cleaning up after these guys, what do you do for work?" she asks.

I want to press, but I don't. I'll get the answers I'm after eventually. But she's given me what I've asked of her so far, so it's only fair that I return the favor.

"I analyze data."

"And Jake?"

"He's a lawyer."

"My boy's a lawyer?"

I nod.

"That's amazing. Dylan must have really stepped up after I left."

I bite my tongue, swallowing down the reply I want to give. It's not my place to tell her the truth about how Jake's dad responded after she abandoned them. Instead, I say, "Jake's incredible."

"And you two are happy?"

I nod, not trusting my voice.

"But you're not married?"

"No."

"And no kids, obviously."

Darting a gaze at Stephano, remembering the joke Jake made just days ago, I shake my head, tears gathering in my eyes.

"Oh, sweetie. It's okay. Considering what's happened, it's for the best, don't you think?"

"Maybe you're right."

"You're done here, aren't you? Come on, let's get you inside."

I let her hook her arm through mine and I walk beside her back to the house. Meekly. Dejectedly. I let her think that I'm weak. Because there's one way to find out who you can trust… and that's to see if they'll kick you when you're down.

CHAPTER 35

Janine sits with me while I eat, though she doesn't touch a bite of food herself. She says she isn't hungry, despite looking like she hasn't had a single decent meal in the decades since she left Gator Glade. Not that I don't understand.

Given the circumstances, my own appetite is nonexistent, my stomach rebelling against the microwave lasagna I force down, telling myself that I need to keep my strength up. But the truth is, I'm mainly just eating something so I have an excuse to sit at the table and retrieve my phone without being too obvious about it.

Because Janine seems reluctant to take her eyes off me, almost like she fears that, if she does, I'll vanish. I'm not used to being watched so closely. And I'm not entirely comfortable with it.

But I can't fault her, either. There's something so hungry about those eyes of hers, too large for her almost painfully thin face. It's as if she's been starved for companionship as much as sustenance. When I put myself in her place and imagine being separated from my family and friends for decades, I have to suspect that I'd probably be the same.

Still, it's a huge relief when she takes me up on my offer of some clean clothes and a shower. Free from her watchful gaze, as soon as I hear the water turn on, I hurry outside.

I feel bad about sneaking around, but it's a necessary evil. I have no idea when I'll be summoned to meet with Nico Castellanos, but I do know that I'm only going to have one chance at getting Jake back. I need to be prepared. And I need to do it without Janine knowing what I'm up to. It's safer for us both that way.

If she notices that I'm slightly out of breath when she comes out of the bathroom, she doesn't let on. And if she doubts my exhaustion as I give a big yawn and declare myself ready to call it a night, it isn't obvious. She just nods and agrees that it would feel good to get some sleep.

Though I offer her the bed, she declines, insisting on taking the couch. The pasta in my stomach churns. I'd rather her in the bedroom. She'd be more secure in there. But I know better than to argue.

Instead, I linger for a moment as she fluffs the pillow I gave her. As soon as I'm sure she's distracted, I make my escape, calling a hasty goodnight as I hurry down the hall. Keeping an eye on her shadow, watching as it bobs on the far wall by the door, I open the door to my room.

But I don't go inside. Instead, I close it, then tiptoe backward through the opposite doorway, crossing the carpet until I feel the cool tiles of Butch's en suite underfoot. Then I take a seat on the edge of the tub to wait in the dark.

Even though I dim the screen on my phone, I slip it inside my shirt just in case. Tucking my head under the fabric, I ignore all the missed calls, voicemails, and text messages, bringing up my email instead. Scrolling past all the subject lines begging me to respond, I open the one sent by Director Jacobson early this morning—the case file for my parents' murders.

There's been something bothering me ever since Janine first told me about Nico Castellanos earlier. She said she didn't go to the cops because he had some of them on his payroll. She said he was a powerful man with a far reach.

But as I study the photographs again, I confirm my earlier impressions of the crime. The man Janine described doesn't match the scene I'm looking at. It's too chaotic and messy for a professional hit.

True, some criminals are smart enough to stage a scene to look like something it's not, but would someone have gone to that much trouble in such a rural area back in the early nineties? I doubt it.

Closing the report, I type his name into a search browser. Opening the first link in the results, I skim the article. Then I read the second hit. Then the third. I read everything I can find about Nico Castellanos, because that's what you're supposed to do, isn't it? Study your opponent?

So I do. I learn that Nico immigrated to America from Greece in the seventies. That he quickly rose to both fortune and power. But while he, in the rare interviews he gave, described himself as a self-made businessman, I find plenty of evidence that supports the truth as Janine told it—he was a drug dealer.

Sure, he may have had his hands in everything from real estate to fashion, but probably only as a way to launder the money he made as, in the words of one journalist, a cocaine cowboy.

Switching over to images, I scroll through photographs of the handsome man. Grinning from in front of a sprawling mansion. Waving from the steps of his private jet. Holding a drink up toward the photographer from the deck of his yacht.

In the last picture, he's shirtless. The way his free

hand gestures toward his body suggests he's proud of his toned physique. His spotless tanned skin. It appears he enjoyed showing himself off just as much as his belongings.

I click the picture of him on the boat and read the caption: *Nico Castellanos shown on his ship, The Devil's Siren, circa 1998*. My heart gives a funny little kick inside my chest. I zoom in.

Sure enough, there, directly beneath where the silver-haired man is standing, on the side of the vessel in fancy script are the words Devil's Siren. And painted right beside the name is the now familiar image of the mermaid with horns.

Even though my gut told me that the crime scene from my parents' murders did not match the profile of this man, this seems like all the proof I need to convince myself that I was wrong. But there are two problems with that.

Before I can address either, there's a long, low creak. It's the door to Butch's room. I'm not alone anymore—I have company.

CHAPTER 36

I force myself to hold still, though the pulse jumping under my skin has me feeling like I might leap out of it. Turning my phone off, I slowly slip my head from the shelter of my shirt and hold my breath, listening carefully. For a long moment there's silence, then the soft shuffle of bare feet across carpet carries to my ears.

My fingers curl into a fist around my phone as I force myself to count to fifty. Then, I get to my feet as quietly as I can, waiting until I've reached the bathroom threshold before flicking the light on.

"Looking for something?" I ask.

Janine jerks, turning to me from her spot on the floor with wide eyes, one hand pressed against her chest. "Cassidy! I was just…"

She looks from me to the flap of carpet she's pulled up, deflating as she realizes that there's no logical way to explain whatever she's doing.

"You knew something bad was going to happen that night," I accuse. I don't bother elaborating on what night I mean. She knows which one I'm talking about.

She holds my eye, her expression turning miserable as she finally nods.

"How?" I ask.

"I don't know. I just had a feeling."

"And that's why I was staying at your place?"

"You were so little. So innocent. I couldn't bear the thought of you getting hurt. So… I offered to watch you. Suggested that your mom take a night off."

"Why didn't you tell her? Or the police?"

Janine digs at a cuticle, ripping a chunk of flesh away. A dark bead of blood rises to the surface, spreading along her nailbed as she says, "I'd been telling her. She didn't want to hear it. And the cops? If I had told them, I would have ended up in the same condition she did."

"But you went there that night. To my parents' house. Why?"

"Because I wanted to try one last time to convince your mom she was making a mistake. But it was too late."

"The killer was already there?"

She nods, swallowing hard.

"But why take pictures?"

"So that I'd have leverage. Just in case."

"In case of what?"

"In case he decided to come after me next."

"Why would he do that?"

She looks like she's going to be sick, the circles under her eyes darker than the shadows surrounding us. "Everyone knew how close your mom and I were. When he didn't find what he was searching for, I knew where he'd turn next."

"To you?"

"Yes," she whispers.

"Which is why you left town?"

Janine nods.

"How'd you get the knife?"

"I followed him when he left. Dug it out of the neighbor's trash."

"And then you hid it here. In Butch's room."

"I didn't know what else to do. Cassidy, you have to

believe me."

"All I *have* to do is wait for word on where and when I'm meeting Castellanos."

"I really don't think you should go. It's too dangerous. That's why I was in here, looking for the pictures. So I could make the exchange for you. It's the least I can do. For you and for Jake." When I shake my head, she licks her lips, glancing around the room nervously. "Do… do you have a gun?"

I give her a startled look. I had thought she had noticed the pistol in my hand when I found her earlier, in the abandoned house. But maybe it had been too dark. Or maybe she had been too scared. Either way, I don't answer the question, instead asking my own.

"You think I need to bring a gun to the meeting?"

"No. You definitely don't want to do that. If you brought a gun with you, all bets would be off. You'd be signing Jake's death warrant."

"Then why'd you ask?"

"Just in case someone came by here to try to take the evidence. I didn't speak with Castellanos directly, just my contact. Who knows how many middlemen the message went through. Or if any of them would decide to try to gain favor by taking care of the problem for him."

"Well, they can try, but it would be a waste of their time. The evidence isn't here."

"Where is it?"

"It's—" I close my mouth, pressing my lips together. "It's probably best that I don't tell you, Janine. Just in case that does happen. But if it does, don't worry. I gave the package to a friend. The place he works at is a fortress. It will be safe there. And if he doesn't hear from me daily until I collect the envelope I gave him, he'll put it in the mail. It will go straight to the FBI."

I hear her gulp from across the room.

"What happened to you the day of the accident?" I ask.

She looks away, wrapping her arms tight around herself.

"Did Castellanos find you?"

She nods.

"I noticed the cuts on your arm. The bruising beneath your fingernails. Were you tortured?"

"Yes," she whispers, tears glinting in her eyes.

"Why?"

"Because he was trying to get me to tell him where the proof was."

"You told him you had pictures?"

"And the knife. I was trying to buy time to think of a way out."

"How did you escape?"

Janine looks out the window as if it isn't boarded up and she can see outside. She starts on a second cuticle, a distant look in her eyes as if she's peering into the past, watching what happened as she tells me.

"When he found me, he was absolutely enraged. I knew he was going to kill me. So I told him I had what he was looking for. That I'd get it for him. But he… he beat me until I told him the truth. That I had no idea where his drugs were. But that there was evidence of what he'd done. And I'd give it to him if he let me loose to get it."

"But he sent someone else to look for it?"

"I'm so sorry, Cassidy. I was weak. I'd seen Butch's obituary in the paper, and I… I had hoped no one would be here when they came to get it."

"I imagine he wasn't happy when they returned empty-handed."

"He was enraged." Her voice breaks as she says,

"Once he found out, he took me outside to shoot me. But I ran. Hid in the swamp until I saw my chance to steal one of their vehicles. I was hoping to get here before anyone got hurt, but I think… I think it was a trap. They followed me."

"And knocked you off the road?"

"Yes."

"Why didn't you tell me who you were then? When I found you in the truck?"

"I was too ashamed. And I didn't want to put you in any more danger than I already had. This is all my fault."

I've heard enough.

"What's done is done," I say. "There's no use blaming yourself. I'm going to get some sleep." I turn off the bathroom light, plunging us into darkness. "You should try to do the same."

I don't so much as glance in her direction as I pass by her on the way to my room. Once inside, I close the door. Then I lock it.

I'm not sure what to make of what she's told me. What to believe. I've spent most of my career looking for patterns, and I'm seeing plenty here.

But it's time to shake things up.

Because this data analyst is pissed—and it's time to change the design. Maybe I wasn't old enough to do anything when they killed my parents, but I'm old enough to do something now.

Taking Jake? Putting themselves on my radar? I'm going to make sure it's the biggest mistake they ever have the chance to make.

CHAPTER 37

I wake with an anxious feeling in my stomach, a mix between Christmas morning when you're a child and having to show up for work after making a very big mistake as an adult. Whatever's going to happen, it will be today. And there are no guarantees that I'll be coming home tonight.

But there's the possibility that I will, and that I'll be bringing Jake with me. That chance, as slim as it seems, is what I'm fighting for.

So when I put my feet on the floor and haul myself out of bed, it's with determination. When I choke down a piece of dry toast and go out to feed the animals, it's with purpose. And as I spot the sheet of paper that's been slipped under my windshield wiper and pull it out, I read it not with fear, but with rage.

It sickens me that they were on my property again. That they escaped unscathed. But I promise myself it's the last time they get away without consequences. One way or another, I'm going to make them pay—for everything.

Hurrying out to the barn, I go through the motions quickly, giving everyone extra food and water, just in case. But before I leave, I slow down and take the time to say goodbye.

I rub salve on the large fatty tumor on the cow's neck

so she won't rub it and make it raw. Scratch the pigs on their rumps like they like. Get the itch behind Daisy's ears. Rub the base of Stephano's horns and give him a snuggle. And the mule? Sam doesn't like to be touched, so I give him compliments instead.

Janine is in the bathroom when I get back inside, which is perfect. I hurry into the kitchen and grab the small paring knife and a slicing knife from the wooden block on the counter, and a plastic sandwich bag from the drawer. I slip the weapons under the covers on my bed before hustling into Butch's en suite and locking the door.

Inching the medicine cabinet from the wall, I remove the bag of evidence I stashed in the hole. Opening the seal, I lay out the Polaroids on the edge of the tub, taking several pictures of each one. I return all but two—the one with the clearest shot of the man's tattoo and the one that best shows my parents bound and gagged with the murder weapon brandished before them.

I use the plastic sandwich bag to remove the knife that was used to murder my parents and put it and the two photographs I'm keeping back in the hole. Flushing the toilet, I return the medicine cabinet to the wall. Running the water in the sink, I clean up all traces of drywall dust.

Then, tucking the package into the waistband of my shorts, careful to keep it concealed beneath my shirt, I exit the en suite and sneak across the hall to my room.

Easing the door shut behind me, I place the plastic bag with the evidence on the bed. Stripping down, I pull on a tighter pair of shorts. A fitted shirt. Slip the paring knife under the bridge of my bra, the tip pointed toward my chin, then check my reflection in the mirror.

I have no doubt that I'll be checked for weapons. I'm hoping that if I wear something that looks impossible to conceal one under, that they'll be lax in their inspection. And the small knife will be almost impossible to detect without completely feeling me up. But either way, I'll be prepared.

Because there's one thing I can say about Butch. Though he wasn't much of a housekeeper—and let's face it, neither am I, the cleaning gene just isn't part of my DNA—the man took exceptional care of his kitchen knives, sharpening them regularly to a razor edge. It's a habit he thankfully didn't abandon as he got older.

I slip the other knife in the baggie with the Polaroids. Unclip the holstered gun from the shorts I'd been wearing, climb up on the bed and place them on top of one of the ceiling fan blades, where I'd already stashed the other two, along with my badge. I put the bag with the evidence into a canvas tote and grab the spare key to Butch's ancient truck.

Then I take one last look around the room, committing it to memory. The stuffed animals on my closet shelf. The drawer on the dresser that will never fully shut. The indent I'd put in the wall when I'd secretly bought a pair of training nunchucks at the mall when I was fourteen.

For so many years, for so many reasons, I avoided this place. Now, I find myself praying that I get to come back to it.

I can't put it off any longer. It's time to go.

Janine is standing in the hall waiting for me as I exit my bedroom. Her eyes move across my face as if she's reading my expression.

"Everything okay?" she asks.

"There was a note on my car. The meeting's been set."

"And?"

Tightening my arm against my side, making sure the

top of the tote bag is pinned shut, I say, "And I have to leave now if I'm going to pick up the evidence and make it on time."

"Cassidy." Her lips press together, but that doesn't still their trembling. Her eyes grow red and watery. "Are you sure?"

"Yes."

"Then I'm going with you. You shouldn't do this alone."

"Janine," I say gently. "I appreciate the offer. Really. You have no idea how much it means to me. But you're in no condition to do… whatever this is. You need to stay here, where it's safe."

She throws her arms around me, a move that takes me by surprise. Though I'm careful to keep my body angled away so she won't feel the knife under my shirt, it's hard not to melt into her embrace.

I could use a good hug right now. A motherly one. There have been far too few of those in my life. I remind myself of why that is.

As she strokes my hair, there's something familiar about it. I get a flash of a playground. Of this woman before me on her knees, crooning in my ear and comforting me after a fall.

I believe that Janine loved me once. Now? It doesn't matter how either of us feel.

"I'm sorry," she whispers in my ear. Then, pulling away, she wipes at a tear that's fallen onto her cheek and gives me a sad smile. "Is there anything I can do?"

"Could you give me an hour's head start, then call the police? Let them know that they're needed out at the Oak Glade trailhead?" Once she nods, I add, "And if I don't come back, could you make sure that the animals are taken care of? There's a rescue over in Homestead that can help."

"Of course."

She gives my arm a squeeze, then follows me to the front door. As our eyes meet one last time before I step outside, a chill runs down my spine. Is it because I've just seen the future? Or a ghost from the past?

CHAPTER 38

My heart matches the strange knocking sound coming from beneath the hood of Butch's truck. With a sudden jolt of panic, I worry that the ancient Ford will break down before I make it to the meeting. I try not to think about what that might mean for Jake.

I've been trying not to think about Jake period. About the gunshot wound in his shoulder, open since he tore his stitches. His rebellious nature which almost guarantees that he's not cooperating with his kidnappers. The way he makes me feel when he looks at me. Or the hole his loss would carve inside my heart.

I have to believe that he's okay. That they wouldn't risk injuring him too severely—or fatally—until they have what they want in their possession. But the kind of people I'm dealing with here aren't always rational.

Power does funny things to people. And that's what this all boils down to, isn't it? Power. The ability to get what you want by force. Not because you deserve it or ask nicely. Not because you make a deal. But by taking the thing that you want, whether it's a person or their life.

My throat tightens, the tears I'm fighting not to shed burning the back of my nose. I rub first my right palm across the stomach of my shirt, then my left, trying to dry them. Draw deep breaths, trying to calm my nerves.

I can do this, I know I can. But I should make a

contingency plan, just in case.

Checking my rearview mirror, I make sure no other vehicles are in sight, then I turn off the road into a small dirt clearing hidden by trees that teenagers used to make out at when I was younger. Pulling out my phone, I type out an email.

In it, I write that I leave everything I own to Jake Walker. And that if he is unable to claim my estate for any reason, that it should go into a trust to ensure the care of every animal currently at the sanctuary, with an equal portion following each animal to the rescue that gives them a new home.

Though I debate for a long minute, the clock is ticking. I don't have the time to think this through any further. I have to go with my gut. I name Director Jacobson as my chosen trustee, then hit send.

There's a chance that when Mallory receives what is essentially my makeshift will, she might panic. When my phone starts blowing up less than five minutes after I've pulled back onto the road, it's confirmed. Instead of answering the call, I place one of my own, to the FBI field office in Miami.

As soon as the operator answers, I give her my identification number and fill in the rest of the details, including the name of the known and dangerous fugitive I'm on my way to meet, the location of the meeting, and directions to the trailhead. Then I request backup and emergency services, knowing that one way or another, we'll need an ambulance, though I'm not sure for who yet—me, the kidnappers, or Jake

"Are you alone out there?"

The disbelief in her tone is clear. She probably thinks this is a crank call. It's certainly not the customary kind they receive.

"Yes. I'm on vacation," I lie. "My supervisor is DIC

Marla Jacobson, out of the Quantico office."

"Do you have eyes on the perp?"

"I'm in pursuit now."

"Alone?"

Though we've already been over this part, I draw a deep breath before calmly saying, "Yes. That's why I'm requesting backup."

"Protocol dictates that you should wait for backup to arrive before pursuing."

"I'm afraid that's not an option. He has a hostage. Do you have all the information you need to dispatch a response?"

"Ma'am—"

"Yes or no?"

"Agent Knox—"

"Yes or no?"

"This is highly unusual."

"Lives are on the line. I need you to come through for me."

With that, I press end. Power off the phone to put a stop to the influx of incoming calls. Lean over and tuck it into the springs under the passenger side of the bench seat.

For the next twenty minutes, I ignore the twisting sensation in my stomach. The way my molars throb. The headache that's begun to hammer behind my eyes.

It grows worse as I turn off the main road and slowly creep down the bumpy dirt path that leads for miles deep into the heart of the hardwood hammocks that form the Everglades forest. Reaching a fork, I stay to the left, following the sign for the Oak Glade trailhead.

The single lane grows narrower the farther I go. The shadows darker as the trees tighten their ranks. It feels like I'm being funneled down a tube. The effect is claustrophobic.

I run through my plan one more time, trying to distract myself. Urge the truck along as the knocking beneath the hood gets louder and more erratic, mirroring my pulse.

"Come on," I whisper. "Come on. You can do it."

It's a pep talk for myself as much as for Butch's pickup.

It feels like I'm stuck in a fever dream, a continuous, never-ending loop of the kind of nightmare where the horror of your own thoughts outperforms anything that could happen in reality. But I know the truth. Imagination is no worse than real life when it comes to the atrocities committed by humans.

Finally, after what seems like an eternity, I spot a car up ahead. The lack of dust trailing behind it lets me know that it's not moving. It's parked facing me, blocking the way forward.

As I get closer, I can see that it's empty. It feels like a trick.

My throat clicks as I try to swallow without any spit. I search the woods around me, watching for motion among the trees. Reluctantly, I come to a stop.

I look for any sign that there's someone nearby, hoping that they were just waiting for me to arrive before showing themselves. Instead, I see another vehicle approaching from behind, kicking up a cloud of dirt as the SUV comes barreling toward me.

I'm penned in, caught between the vacant car in front of me, the one racing up behind me, and the trees lining the sides of the narrow lane. There's nowhere to go. I'm trapped.

CHAPTER 39

The oversized SUV approaches way too fast, sending up a billowing shroud of dust as it comes to a sudden halt about twenty yards from where I've stopped. I study it in my rearview mirror, but the windows are tinted too dark to see through.

There could be any number of people in the vehicle. I wait for one of them to emerge. When that fails to happen, it becomes clear that they're waiting for me to make the first move.

I unlatch my seatbelt and crack open the door. Suck in a deep breath, trying to banish the lightheaded feeling that's claimed me. Then carefully step down from the truck, shoving the key into my pocket.

The air is thick and humid, scented by the dirt still settling back to the earth. A layer immediately coats my body, mixing with the sweat that's sprung to the surface of my skin. Walking to the back of the vehicle, I stop and wait, swallowing hard as three doors of the SUV open.

I don't recognize any of the men who get out. None of them, as far as I can see, have a horned mermaid tattoo. Which means I have no idea who I'm dealing with here, or why.

The man who emerges from the front passenger seat crosses his arms and leans them on the top of the doorframe. "You've got something that belongs to me," he calls across the distance. My eyes flick between him and the two other men, trying to gauge the biggest threat. "Where is it?"

"Where's Jake?" I counter. "I want to see him first."

The guy who spoke must be the one in command. He nods to the driver of the SUV, a pale man with giant ears. Dumbo opens the door behind him and leans inside. There's some scuffling and a loud grunt as he drags a fourth person from the vehicle. His hands are bound at the wrists in front of him. There's a hood drawn over his head.

The sight of it evokes the chemical stench of burlap, the coarse feel of the fabric as it was pulled down over my face. The memory makes my legs weak.

I shove the feeling down deep to deal with later. Assuming there is a later. If not, I guess I won't have to deal with the trauma of that or any of the rest of this. Look, a silver lining.

Forcing myself back to the moment, I watch as the big-eared goon tosses a rope over the limb of a tree that overhangs the narrow lane. He threads it through the zip tie binding the hooded man's wrists and pulls tight, until the man's hands are raised so high over his head that he has to struggle to keep his feet flat on the ground.

I try not to think about the pain Jake must be in, with his wounded shoulder torqued up like that. Because even with the hood on, I can tell that it's him. Even if he wasn't wearing the same clothes I'd last seen him in, albeit much dirtier now, I'd recognize his body, the way he moves.

Despite that, I say, "That could be anyone. Take the hood off."

The man who tied him up glances over his shoulder at the one in charge, who nods. He tugs the hood off Jake's head.

A tormented expression contorts Jake's face as our eyes meet across the distance. "Get out of here, Cassie," he yells. "Run!"

I shake my head softly. "I can't do that."

"Cassie, huh," the guy in command says. "That's a pretty name for a pretty girl. A *very* pretty girl."

I ignore the leering look he gives me, this man who's probably old enough to be my father, and instead try to send positive thoughts to Jake that everything is going to be okay. I don't know if things like that work, but what else am I going to do? Admit to myself what a hopeless situation this is?

The man in charge points to the guy who'd been seated behind him, a bald guy with heavy jowls. "My lucky friend here is going to search you for weapons. Then we'll finish our business."

Though he beckons me forward, I don't move, making the bald man cross the entire distance instead of meeting him halfway. When he reaches me, I hold my arms out to my sides.

I battle the urge to resist as he runs his skeevy hands down my sides. Across my stomach. He's taking his time, making it last too long. One of his hands reaches into my pocket, removing the key to the truck, and slips it into his own. The other trails down the front of my shorts, cupping my crotch.

"Get your hands off her," Jake yells. I see him tugging at his bonds, trying to free himself, but it's in vain. He looks paler than he did a moment ago.

The bald man groping me laughs. "You're not exactly in the position to have a vote in this, boss."

He tightens his grip until it's painful. I clench my jaw, refusing to wince. Showing weakness of any kind right now is not an option.

"All right, let's wrap this up," the man in charge

yells.

Baldie drops his hands from my body, though he stays behind me, in my blind spot.

"I showed you mine." The head honcho points to Jake. "Now show me yours. Where's the gift you brought me?"

"In the truck. Under the passenger floor mat."

The big-eared guy beside Jake strides over, though it's the driver's side door that I hear creak open behind me. There's the sound of rustling. Of the seat moving.

He rounds to the passenger side, continuing his search of the vehicle. The glove compartment slams shut. The tailgate groans as it's lowered. Bangs as it's raised.

Then the man reappears with the bag in hand. I watch as he walks it over to his boss, who drops his casual pose as he grabs the package greedily, holding the plastic baggie up in front of his face as he looks inside.

My heart threatens to hammer its way through the wall of my chest. Is he counting the number of Polaroids inside? Will he notice the lack of blood on the knife?

Finally, he tosses the package inside the SUV, then looks at me, wearing a nasty smile as his eyes meet mine. "It was nice doing business with you."

The driver rounds the vehicle, climbing back behind the wheel. The guy in command steps up onto the runner board to haul himself inside.

Though I should feel relieved, I'm filled with a growing sense of worry instead. This was too easy. There's no way they're going to drive off and leave me and Jake here unscathed.

Then from behind me, Dumbo asks, "What should I do with her?"

The man in charge grins wider, then says, "She looks like fun. Bring her with us, we'll have ourselves a little party."

An arm loops around me, squeezing so tight that the air is crushed from my lungs. It's all I can do not to gag between that and the obscene things my captor whispers he's going to do to me. My stomach heaves against his iron grip as he runs his slimy tongue along my cheek. This is it. The moment I didn't want to wait for.

CHAPTER 40

All I can hear is the sound of my pulse as I'm lifted off my feet. I draw shallow breaths, struggling to fill my lungs. Then, with all of my strength, I throw my weight forward. My captor laughs as he rises up on my back.

My legs tremble, as much with adrenaline as the added burden of his weight. But they only have to hold another moment.

Reaching under my shirt, I grab the handle of the tiny paring knife. Pull it free so fast that my skin burns with the slice of the blade. But there are worse things to suffer. And I'm determined not to experience any of them today.

I slam the knife into his thigh all the way to the hilt, stabbing into the tendon above his knee. Throw everything I have into giving it a twist. He howls. His breathing is loud, labored as he curses, yanking me by the hair. My scalp stings as the roots threaten to rip free.

It's not nice of him, considering I could have aimed for his femoral artery. Out here, so far from help, that would be lethal. But judging by the sound of the snap as I jam my elbow into him as hard as I can, catching him in the throat, and the way he suddenly goes limp, releasing me as he crumples to the ground, I may have dealt him a fatal blow after all. I'd try to muster up an ounce of sympathy, but there's no time.

Falling to my knees, I turn my torso parallel to the ground as I reach under the truck and rip the pump action shotgun from where I'd taped it to the ledge created by the bar that holds the hitch mount, suddenly thankful for the time I was sixteen and spun in the mud, losing control and catching the bumper on a tree, ripping it off. It was a crucial lesson to learn—in more ways than one.

Funny how the memory of something like that sticks with you until you need it. Like when you're searching for a place to stash a weapon that no one would ever think to check.

Standing, I face the SUV. The man in charge curses when he sees what I hold in my hands. He dives inside the vehicle.

The engine revs. But it surges forward, not back. My stomach lurches as I realize what the driver intends. He's coming for me. And Jake is caught between us, unable to escape.

Racing toward the approaching vehicle, I dart to the side, into the wood line. Raise the shotgun to my shoulder and fire a series of shots at the engine block as quickly as I can pump the weapon until the sound of the motor ceases. To my relief, the SUV quickly loses momentum, drifting to a stop before it reaches Jake.

Wasting no time, I stalk forward, weaving as I stick to the shelter of the trees, ready to fire again at a moment's notice, though I hope I won't have to. It took five rounds to stop the car. I only have one left—and two assailants remain.

As I watch, the back hatch rises up, appearing over the rear of the vehicle. I hear the soles of the men's shoes striking the dirt as they run, though I catch only a brief glimpse of them as they disappear into the forest on the opposite side of the lane as me.

If I were them, I'd be positioning myself behind a

big tree and waiting for a clear shot to take me out. But they're not me. They're the cowards who made the huge mistake of underestimating a very angry woman.

Still, I'm careful, keeping the shotgun against my shoulder and aimed in their general direction as I approach Jake. I blink away tears as I take him in—his face mottled with dark bruises, the skin beneath ashen and slick with sweat. His clothes are stained with blood and grime.

As much as I long to touch him, hold him, reassure myself that he's okay, there isn't time. I force a swallow past the lump in my throat to talk.

"I can't reach the rope to untie you," I say.

"Just leave me, Cassie. You need to get out of here while you have the chance."

"I'm not going anywhere without you. I'm going to shoot the rope. But if they were counting my shots, they might know that I only have one slug left. We'll need to run as soon as you're free. Can you do that?'

"Don't worry about me."

"I didn't come out here to go home alone. Can you do it or not?"

He draws a deep breath before giving a single nod of his head. "I'll be right behind you. I promise."

I have to rise up on my tiptoes in order to press the end of the barrel to the rope, which means I can't shoulder the weapon properly. I'm going to have one heck of a bruise tomorrow. But as long as there is a tomorrow, and both Jake and I are a part of it, I don't care.

Preparing to do my best to maintain my balance, I pull the trigger. The butt of the shotgun slams into my clavicle. Knocked backward, I fall, striking my tailbone painfully against the ground. Immediately, Jake's bound hands pull me to my feet. Then, we run to Butch's truck.

"Get in," I say.

Popping open the door to the fuel tank, I catch the extra slugs I stashed there before they can fall. Opening the chamber, I reload the shotgun tube, then grab the spare truck key and remaining ammo. Bending, I confirm the bald man is dead as I wrench the knife free from his thigh, then climb into the cab.

"Hold out your hands."

Even after I slice through the zip tie that binds his wrists, it stays in place. Jake hisses as I gently pull it free from the raw, weeping wounds it made. He rubs at the indents as I put the key in the ignition and turn. We stay low, both keeping our heads barely above the dash as I put the truck in reverse and creep toward the vehicle blocking the lane behind us.

"Are you okay?" I ask Jake.

"I'm fine."

The strain in his tone would suggest that's not entirely true, as would his coloring, but I don't argue. He's here. We'll work on whatever medical care he needs later.

"What are we going to do?" he asks as I come to a stop just in front of the disabled SUV.

"I'm going to put it in neutral. We'll push it until we reach one of the turnouts and can get by."

"Let me do it."

"I'm already on the right side. It'll take longer, be more of a risk if you do it."

He gives me a look that lets me know he wants to disagree. I reach out, gingerly running my fingers across his bruised cheek. Smile for the first time in what feels like years.

"You know how to use this thing?" I ask, gesturing to the shotgun between us.

When he nods, I slide the small back window open.

"You can cover me. I'll be quick."

He catches me as I move to turn away, his hand cupping the back of my head. He presses his forehead against mine. "I love you, Cassie. I always have."

"My heart has always belonged to you, Jake Walker."

He gives me a sad smile and brushes a quick kiss against my lips before releasing me.

"I'll be right back," I promise.

"You better be."

I pretend like my nerves aren't as frayed as the rope I shot through to release Jake as I crack the door open and slip outside. Stay low as I make my way to the end of the truck bed. Hold my breath and listen. Then, I make my move.

CHAPTER 41

My skin bristles as I dart to the open door of the SUV. I tell myself that I'll only be out here a minute, that the eyes I feel on me are imaginary as I lean inside and try to shift the gear from drive to neutral. But it doesn't move.

I glance around, trying to convince myself I'm not being watched. That someone's not waiting for me to make myself vulnerable to seize the opportunity to strike. My stomach bubbles as I weigh my options.

The decision is made in an instant. As much as I don't like it, there's only one choice if I plan to get us out of here. I'm going to have to get in the SUV.

My heart feels like it's rising up my throat as I worry that this won't work without a key fob. Swallowing it down, I climb into the driver's seat and push my foot against the brake. Hold my breath as I try moving the gearshift. Release it on a sigh of relief as the lever moves into neutral.

I hurry back to the truck, Jake and I exchanging tense looks as I climb back inside and lock the door. He looks even paler than he did before. I need to get him out of here.

Easing my foot down on the gas, I brace myself as the metal of the truck's rear bumper meets against the plastic coating of the SUV's front one. The tires spin for a moment once contact is made and then we slowly start making progress backward.

"Did they leave my phone in here?" I ask, watching the rearview mirror, making sure to keep the vehicles aligned. "It was up in the springs under the passenger seat."

Jake leans forward slowly, feeling around beneath him. His hand emerges with the device and a grease stain a moment later.

"Yes."

"Great. The lockscreen's disabled. Can you turn it on for me and call the last number I dialed?"

"You want me to put it on speaker?"

"Please."

The line rings twice before it's answered. I don't even let the receptionist finish her spiel before I launch in.

"This is Special Agent Cassidy Knox again. Two assailants are now on foot along the Oak Glade trail. A third is down. You'll find him on the lane leading left from the fork of the main road near an abandoned sedan. Tell me you have backup on their way?"

"I do, Agent Knox. ETA should be less than ten minutes. Can I get a description of who we're looking for?"

"White males, one looks mid-forties, the other closer to sixty. What about an ambulance?"

"At the turnoff to the trailhead, waiting for backup to escort them in."

"Tell them we're on our way. We'll meet them there."

"Stay safe."

"Thank you."

Jake presses the button to end the call and turns to face me. I can feel his eyes as I continue to watch behind me as we trundle along. The fork comes into view.

"Don't you think you should have waited for backup as well?" he asks. "Cassie. Seriously. Do you know how lucky you got back there?"

"I do," I say softly. Then, louder, "Get down."

We both duck low in our seats.

"Who is it?" Jake asks. "Is it the other agents you're expecting?"

"No," I say sadly.

"Then who?"

I don't respond, not having the heart to tell him. He cranes his neck, watching in the side mirror as we approach the other vehicle. Before we reach it, two men dart from the woods, both hopping into the back seat of the car. I briefly debate using the SUV as a battering ram but decide against it. It isn't necessary.

I make eye contact with the driver through the lowered window.

"Mom?" Jake asks quietly. Then, rolling his window down, he sticks his head out and yells the word. "Mom!"

She raises her hand and mouths his name. Then she turns in a tight circle and speeds down the road away from us.

"You've got to catch up with them," Jake urges.

I press the gas, changing direction as soon as we reach the fork and we're free of the SUV. Jake raises his window as the dust stirred up by the chase fills the car. He groans as we bounce in our seats, hitting the pits in the dirt road with bone-jarring force.

Glancing over to check that he's okay, I see that his skin has grown grayer, his sweating more profuse. I start to slow, afraid of what injuries are getting aggravated, but he waves me forward. I do my best to accommodate, the truck tires eating the distance between the two vehicles, the knocking under the hood growing into a frantic banging.

"Isn't that your car?" he asks as we catch up to them, the truck, as old as it is, a better match for the rough terrain.

"Yes."

He glances at me. Flinches, cursing, as the windshield cracks.

I stomp on the brakes as a second gunshot rings out, shattering the driver's side-view mirror. We're left watching from a standstill as they speed into the distance ahead.

"What now?" Jake asks. "Do we just let them get away?"

"We only let them think they do."

"What do you mean?"

I turn to face him.

"When you were taken, I knew I had to find your mom. That she would have the answers I was looking for. Namely, who to contact to get you back."

He slumps in his seat, looking defeated. "She's the one who had them take me?" His voice sounds weak. Strained.

I put my hand on his. "No. I'm certain that she didn't. The fear in her eyes when I told her they had you was real."

"But?"

"But that doesn't mean I trusted her. She helped me arrange this meeting. And she genuinely seemed to want to help. But I couldn't take any chances. I didn't know what kind of trouble she was in, or how that might affect her behavior. So I didn't let her know what I was up to. Not my plan, or that I was FBI, or that I had a backup in place just in case."

I don't tell him the whole truth. Not how I'd noticed her favoring the same leg as the assailant who broke into my house and slammed me into the wall.

Or about how I realized that there was no flash from a window in the pictures she admitted she took, and that the distance between the camera and my parents was too short for the photographer not to be in the room with them—there's no zoom on a Polaroid.

And though the call my cell phone recorded her making, the one to arrange the meeting, was cryptic enough that I could believe she wasn't involved in what was going on, there was the fact that Nico Castellanos was already middle-aged when my parents were killed. Despite Janine talking about him as if he were still alive, he's not. According to the obituary I found online, he died several weeks ago. He also didn't have a tattoo.

Unlike Anthony "Tony" Bianchi. Using a photo I took of the horned mermaid from one of the Polaroids, Google Lens helped me identify the true owner of the tattoo last night when I should have been trying to sleep. But I didn't need any help identifying the woman smiling on his arm. We were under the same roof.

Maybe I'll share all this with Jake in time, but there's one thing I vow to never tell him, and that's that in one of the two photos I kept, still hidden in the wall behind the medicine cabinet in Butch's bathroom, my mom's frightened eyes weren't on the man with the knife in his hand, but to his right, staring directly into the lens.

For whatever reason, Janine didn't just know my parents were going to be murdered. She was there when it happened, documenting it instead of stopping it.

Right now, though, I do my best to spare his feelings. "I don't think she had a choice. I think she got in too deep with some dangerous people and that she's been doing whatever she has to do to survive ever since."

His expression tightens as he says, "You should have turned her in. She could have hurt you."

Maybe he's right. If I had turned Janine in, then Jake would have a chance to see her. He'd know where to go to talk to her, to ask all the questions I'm sure he must have after the last thirty-plus years. And I'd be able to press for the truth about my parents. But I couldn't do that.

Staring down at my lap, I say, "I couldn't risk not getting you back. Besides, it's coming."

"What do you mean?"

"I activated my car as a hot spot and took one of the Wi-Fi surveillance cameras from the barn, put it on the front of the rearview mirror. It will show everything they see. Every turn they make and street sign they pass."

"Can we access the feed from the camera inside the car from your phone? Does it have sound?"

"I'm not sure that's a good idea."

But he's already jabbing at the screen. A moment later, the app for the security system appears. Each camera is represented by an image from the last clip played from it. The one I placed in the car is obvious from the test I ran.

"Jake."

I reach over and take his hand before he can hit play. His fingers curl tight around mine. They feel cold despite the warmth in the cab as the air conditioning in Butch's old truck struggles to fight against the heat outside.

"It's okay, Cassie. I can handle it."

But he shouldn't have to. Still, I don't argue as he gently pulls free from my grasp and presses play. A pop sounds through the device's speaker, followed by another.

Janine's voice sounds shrill and staticky as she shrieks, "What are you doing?"

"Chill. I'm just wrapping up loose ends."

"Well, stop! That's my son in there!"

The sounds were the shots they fired at us. There must be a delay in the footage.

"That's your kid?"

"Yes. Stop shooting at them."

I glance at Jake. His breathing has grown shallow and labored, his skin so pale it's almost translucent. He really doesn't look good.

There's a pause before the phone's speaker emits a, "Whoops."

"What do you mean, 'whoops?'" Janine asks.

"You're not going to like it," the man warns her.

"Jake?" I ask.

His eyes are only half open as they meet mine. They flutter, rolling back in his head as he slumps limply in his seat. And though my voice as I yell his name is every bit as loud as the gunshots were earlier, he doesn't react at all.

CHAPTER 42

I stare at Jake for a horrified instant before I spring into action. Pulling my legs up onto the seat, I crawl toward him. The truck, still in gear, starts to slowly roll forward. Cursing, I kick my left foot down, pinning my toes against the brake pedal as I stretch across the cab.

My hands shake as I reach forward. Jake's flesh is icy beneath my fingertips as I press them to his neck. His pulse is weak and thready. I've got to get us out of here, to the ambulance at the trailhead.

I never should have slowed down, much less come to a stop. I could see that Jake was injured. I should have made him lie down and kept on driving, let the other car shoot away until they were out of ammo. Instead, I wasted vital time.

"What'd you do?" Janine's panicked voice fills the cab of the truck. The video feed from the car is still playing, though I can barely hear it over the mounting panic in my head.

Grabbing Jake by his shoulders, I pull him with me as I return to the driver's seat, flooring the gas before I've even gotten settled. I snap forward, catching myself against the wheel with one hand as I hold Jake in place with the other.

As we careen down the dirt road, I glance over, trying to convince myself that he'll be okay. Do a double-take as I notice the blood-soaked seat where he'd been sitting.

"What'd you do?" Janine asks again.

Groping blindly, I search for the source of his bleeding. My hand runs over his chest, his shoulder, his arm, his stomach. Finding nothing, I lean over as far as I dare, feeling for the bottom of his shirt. It's drenched, blood wringing from the fabric, seeping between my fingers as I yank it up.

Finally, I feel the slow pulse of blood against my palm. My gaze darts back and forth between Jake and the road ahead as I assess the wound on the back of his hip.

From my phone's speaker, a man's voice says, "I needed to take a little of the fight out of him, so I gave him a little stick before I handed him over is all."

A stab wound. Which means he's been slowly bleeding out all this time.

The tirade of curse words coming from Janine's mouth matches my own internal dialogue. I punch the steering wheel, gritting my teeth against my tears and fears. My frustration that he didn't tell me what had happened.

No doubt he thought he was staying silent to keep me safe. Instead, it's going to lead to me doing something really stupid. Applying as much pressure as I can against the small puncture, I practically stand on the gas pedal, pressing it against the floor.

"Aw, come on, Janine. It's not like I knew he was your kid. Besides, this whole thing was your idea. It's not my fault that it went south."

"And I suppose you think that it's mine?" Janine asks. "The old man is dead. How was I supposed to know that there'd be someone in the house with a gun?"

I swallow hard. Janine knew Butch had died, but not that I'd moved back home to take over the sanctuary. If only I had stayed in my room the night they broke in, they would have left with what they wanted and none of this would have happened.

"You're going to be okay," I tell Jake. It has to be true. I try to do the math, figuring out how long he's been bleeding, how much blood he's lost, whether the wound is over a critical area like his kidney or intestine, but I keep getting sidetracked by the conversation playing through my phone.

"You think it was fun for me," Janine continues, "when that little fancy-shoed traitor, Kenny, knocked me out and brought me to Tony? Do you have any idea how pissed he was?"

"I can imagine," one of the men says. "If my girlfriend had decided to blackmail me for some murders she talked me into committing, I'd be pissed, too."

The lump in my throat grows even larger. I can't believe it's true, that it was Janine's idea to kill my parents. But she doesn't deny it.

"He'd be nothing without me," she hisses. "He was just one of Castellanos's grunts when I met him. If I hadn't found those bricks of coke, someone else would have and they wouldn't have given any of them back. Or found him a patsy to frame for the kilos we kept. All these years I've helped him seize opportunities he wasn't brave enough to take on his own until he climbed the ranks to second in command, and then as soon as Nico croaked and Tony took over, he decided he was done with me? No."

"I'm just saying I understand, is all."

"Well, we have the leverage I need to get him to ante up now. And after what he did to me, he'll pay double unless he wants me to turn it over to the cops. Triple if it turns out you killed my kid."

I glance at Jake, confirming he's still unconscious

and that he didn't hear how callously his mother just spoke about his possible death. That she planned to profit from it, if it happened.

Looking back up, I ease off the gas reluctantly, just enough to keep the tires on the road around a sharp curve. Loose gravel pings against the sides of the truck. And then there it is. The trailhead parking lot, but more importantly, the waiting ambulance.

Skidding to a halt, I punch the horn, drawing the EMTs' attention. I know they're supposed to be waiting for the Feds to get here to secure the scene and make sure it's safe, but we don't have time for that. Jake doesn't have time for that.

As their eyes meet mine through our windshields, I pray that they'll take the risk and help. And as their doors open, I burst into tears of relief.

"It's going to be okay," I tell Jake as I kick my own door open. I know I'm babbling, but I can't help it. "Help is here. You're going to be okay."

There's never been a sound sweeter to my ears than that of the gurney as it clatters across the dirt toward us.

"He was stabbed," I say as they reach us. "The back of his right hip. About twenty minutes ago."

Assessing the situation, one of the paramedics rounds the truck to Jake's side, opening the door and climbing into the cab. The other runs back to the ambulance, returning seconds later with some hemostatic gauze. I answer their questions as they dress the wound and take Jake's vitals.

The grim look they exchange isn't lost on me.

But I refuse to give up hope. I will Jake to hold on, to fight as they gently remove him from the truck and onto the gurney. I hold my breath, unable to breathe, doing my best to stay out of the way as they work to stabilize him.

The sound of engines approaches. The lot fills with dust tinged in alternating shades of red and blue from strobing lights. I know backup has finally arrived, but I can't bring myself to look, unable to take my eyes off Jake even for an instant.

I inhale sharply as the paramedics finally break into motion, hurrying him to the ambulance. I jog behind, anxious to keep up.

"Agent Knox."

I ignore whoever's calling me. Hover as the gurney is secured. Lift my foot onto the rear step, grabbing onto the handle to lift myself up as the EMT waves me inside.

"Agent Knox."

A hand seizes me by the elbow. "Let go." I shrug my arm, trying to free myself, but they tighten their grip, keeping me in place.

"We have to get going," the EMT says impatiently. He leans forward, reaching to pull the door shut. "We'll take good care of him," he promises.

I open my mouth to insist that I'm going with them, when I'm jerked backward. The doors close. I watch helplessly as the ambulance speeds off, leaving me behind.

"You know protocol."

I wheel around, finding myself face to face with Agent Richards.

"We need you to debrief us on the situation."

A fire ignites inside me. One fueled by pure rage.

This is the man who thought that Jake had left because he didn't want to be in my life. Who turned his back and left me to do this alone. Now, Jake might be dying. And I won't be there when he needs me most because Agent Richards wants an update?

I know I need to calm down so I can get in Butch's truck and drive myself to the hospital, but the smug look on Agent Richards' face isn't helping. So I take it off.

CHAPTER 43

The first punch is just a pop to the nose. It's meant to wound Agent Richards' pride more than to cause actual harm. He yelps, hands cupped around the injury as blood sprays from his nostrils. The problem is that I hadn't expected this small act of retribution to feel so good.

I've never inflicted violence on anyone when it wasn't necessary before. It's certainly not something I've ever enjoyed. But there's no denying that in this instance, I do. So much so that I find myself grabbing him by the collar of his shirt so abruptly that his hands fly out to his sides for balance.

Though I see his colleagues reach toward their holsters, I don't let that stop me. I release his shirt as I deliver the second punch, one that sends him flying backward. The other agents have drawn their weapons now, have them aimed at me.

"Whoa, whoa, whoa."

One of them gestures for the others to relax as she steps between me and Agent Richards. I was done with the man, anyway. I don't have any more time to waste on him. Turning on my heel, I march toward the truck.

The redheaded agent falls into step beside me. "Listen. I understand that you're upset, and rightfully so, but we do need you to fill us in on what happened."

I grab my phone from the passenger side footwell. "Here." Shoving the device into her hands, I slam the door shut and brush past her on the way to the driver's side. "I've disabled the screen lock."

Drawing a shaky breath, I add, "The perps are in a vehicle registered in my name. I have a surveillance camera running via hotspot. It'll show you where they're headed. A copy is uploading to the cloud. Watch it and you should have everything you need to prosecute."

I climb behind the wheel and reach for the door. She grabs it before I have a chance to shut it.

"Hold on a sec," she says, holding her hands up in a pacifying gesture. "Let me drive you to the hospital. Please. You can fill me in on the way."

The memory of the noises the truck made, how hard I pushed it once I discovered Jake was injured, make me pause.

"We'll make it there faster with the lights and sirens running," she promises.

I step down from the vehicle. She beckons to a couple of her colleagues, tossing her keys to one of them as she opens the rear door of the SUV for me. I give her a warning look before getting in.

"Which way?" the driver asks.

"West. Follow the signs toward Naples."

The redheaded agent slides into the other side of the back seat. She passes my cell to the man riding shotgun. I watch as he plugs a headset into the phone and brings up the video feed.

"There's a delay," I tell him.

"How long?"

"I'm not positive. Maybe five minutes."

"What's the login for remote access?"

"Agenthardknox@gmail.com. The password is ZebraGuard, capital Z, capital G."

He arches an eyebrow at me but doesn't comment as he relays the information I gave him via text. I shift my gaze to the speedometer. It reads eighty and we're still accelerating. Satisfied that they're keeping their end of the bargain, I settle back in my seat, exhausted.

The woman beside me gives me a tense smile. "Long day, huh?"

Not having the energy for small talk, I don't respond.

"Agent Amy Gellar," she says.

"Cassidy Knox."

"Tell me who we're dealing with here, Agent Knox."

"The driver is Janine Walker."

"You know her?"

"I did when I was little. She was friends with my parents before she had them killed."

A muscle twitching under her left eye is her only reaction. "Is there already a warrant out for her arrest?"

"No. No one knew. She took off right after. Her own husband thought she was dead. But if you listen to the footage, there's a full confession."

"Why'd she do it?"

I wish I could say I don't know, but I suspect that maybe I do. That the truth was buried somewhere among the lies in the story Janine told me about my mom. Only, I doubt my mom had any idea what was really going on.

"From what I could piece together, thirty-three years ago she got her hands on some cocaine belonging to Nico Castellanos."

The driver releases a low whistle, no doubt familiar with the name.

"I don't know if she knew Tony Bianchi beforehand, or if he was a connection she made after, but they kept some of the drugs. Blamed what was missing on my parents and returned the rest to Nico. Bianchi already worked for him—he had Nico's horned mermaid tattooed on him in the pictures Janine took when they committed the murders."

"You have photographic evidence?"

"I kept two of the Polaroids. The rest are in the bag I had to exchange to get Jake back, but I switched out the knife, so—"

"You have the murder weapon?"

I nod.

"Where?"

"At my home. It's the Gator Glade Sanctuary off the Tamiami. The knife and the Polaroids are in the wall behind the medicine cabinet in the master bathroom. Janine probably left the door unlocked, but if you send someone to recover the evidence, tell them to watch out for my goat."

"Goat?"

"It's an animal sanctuary, Agent Gellar. His name's Stephano and he's an escape artist. If he hears people, he's going to want to meet them. I'm trusting you to make sure he stays safe."

"Noted. Go on."

"There's not much more to it. Janine helped Bianchi climb up the ranks. I guess when Castellanos died a few weeks back, Bianchi took over for him. But he must have done something to piss Janine off, because she decided to blackmail him with the evidence she'd hidden in my grandfather's house. The only problem is I was there when they broke in."

"Who's they? Are they in the car with her?"

"No. The man who broke into my place with her was some guy named Kenny. She killed him. I can tell you where to find the body when we get to the hospital, it's not far from there, a couple of streets over. You'll find video from hospital security showing the man trying to abduct me from the parking garage. And in my surveillance files, of him and Janine breaking into my house. You'll be able to match his shoes to those on the corpse."

"Sounds like you've had your hands full." Agent Gellar gives me a look that's half disbelief. "How many people were you up against back there?"

"On the trail? Three. One of them is still out there. The other two are in the car with Janine."

"Do we need to be worried about the straggler getting away?"

"He's not going anywhere."

I lean forward as we turn off the main road, onto the street that leads to the hospital.

"What about the guy in the ambulance? How's he connected to all this?"

"They took him as leverage to get what they wanted from me."

As we pull into the parking lot, she says, "What I don't understand, Agent Knox, is why you didn't ask for help with all this?"

"Why don't you ask Agent Richards about that?" I sigh in response to the look Agent Gellar gives me, then say, "The man in the ambulance? He was my best friend growing up. He's also Janine's son."

I clear my throat to steady my voice.

"When Agent Richards found out that Jake and I had become romantically involved during the few weeks I've been back in town, and that Janine had reappeared, he was sure that Jake had staged his own disappearance to escape me because things were moving too fast."

As we pull up to a stop sign, I open my door and hop out before anyone has a chance to react.

"So in response to your question, Agent Gellar, I

tried. Sometimes, the only choice you have is to handle things yourself." Turning to the driver, I say, "When you leave the lot, head straight for two blocks, then take a left. Look for the abandoned house. Go around back, you'll find the plywood that covered the back door off. The body is just inside, on the kitchen floor."

Then I turn and bolt for the emergency room door, praying that I've gotten here in time.

CHAPTER 44

I bolt upright, heart pounding as I gaze, disoriented, around the unfamiliar room. Fear tightens its icy fingers around me as I remember what happened. And why I'm here.

Disappointment with myself warms my skin as I realize that I must have fallen asleep. It's instantly replaced by worry. Because something must have woken me.

Silently, I slip from the hard plastic chair in the corner. My eyes lock on the door, watching as the handle depresses. It opens with a soft click, a sliver of light spilling into the room.

My hands curl into fists as I position myself between it and the hospital bed. I swallow at the hard knot that's formed in my throat. Dread sours my stomach.

I glance at Jake, still out cold, before returning my focus to the door. The gap grows excruciatingly slowly, as if whoever's on the other side is afraid to enter. Or preparing to attack.

It doesn't matter how many assurances I've been given that we're safe. They're all promises from people I don't trust, which makes them worthless.

Maybe once Jake wakes, I'll be able to relax, but until that happens, it's up to me to keep him safe. Which means no matter how exhausted I am, I can't let my guard down, not yet.

I have to stay ready to fight.

Though the FBI was able to use the video from the surveillance camera to track Janine and the two men who got away, the time lag proved to be a downfall. They arrived at the marina just as the fugitives' boat was speeding off. The Coast Guard was called immediately, but by the time they rallied and reached the area, it was too late. The trio was gone.

Which means, for the time being at least, they're still out there. They could be on an island in the Caribbean by now. But they could also be hiding in any of the dozens of private boathouses within miles of where they put in. There's no way to know until they're found.

And though I doubt they'd risk coming back so soon, I'm not taking any chances.

Because the conversation recorded by the camera I'd planted in my car provided enough incriminating evidence to send all three of the fugitives—as well as Tony Bianchi— to prison.

Although the drug kingpin has been arrested and charged with my parents' murders, there's no telling yet how far his reach extends. We know he has at least one dirty cop in his pocket. What if they tell him who was responsible for his arrest?

These people are hardened criminals. They've done horrible things. If they ever figure out what I did, I have no doubt they'll seek revenge. And the best way to hurt me is in this room, completely defenseless.

Jake woke for mere minutes when the anesthesia wore off after surgery to repair the stab wound he received, which had nicked his right kidney. He was up just long enough to give me a sleepy, lopsided smile and say, "You're here."

Then he fell back asleep. He's been unconscious

ever since, not even stirring when the nurse came in to check the dressings on his wounds and his vitals.

I've come so close to losing him already. To being completely alone in this world once again. Knowing he's so vulnerable is terrifying.

I wish I had someone I could trust to help keep him safe while he recovers.

It's not that I'm concerned I can't handle it on my own. If there's one thing this experience over the past week has taught me, it's that I can trust myself again, even under pressure.

But it would be nice if I didn't have to do it alone. Eventually, I'm going to need to rest.

My stomach feels like it's climbing up my throat, my muscles bunching into knots as I watch the door warily. My vision blurs, my dry, gritty eyes longing to close. Why hasn't the person who opened it shown themselves? What are they waiting for?

Out of patience, I creep forward. Just as I get close enough to reach out and grab the handle, it swings open the rest of the way. I stumble back with a gasp, one hand pressed to my chest, trying to calm my frantic heart as I stare in disbelief at the person standing before me.

"Director Jacobson."

She gives me a tight smile, then looks past me into the room. Glancing over my shoulder, I follow her gaze to Jake's still form.

"Is that him?" Mallory Chan hisses from behind her in what has to be the loudest whisper known to womankind. "Girl, he's gorgeous!"

I look at the chair where I'd been sleeping in the corner, making sure that I'm not still in it, that this isn't some weird dream, then turn to face them both, still half dazed with surprise.

"What are you doing here?" I ask, running my palms

over my grungy shorts and T-shirt, suddenly aware that I'm in dire need of a shower.

"Well, when one of my favorite agents refused to answer my calls and texts, I got worried. Then, after reading the email you sent Mallory, when you still wouldn't respond, I contacted Agent Richards to see if he could give me an update on what was going on… Maybe I panicked a bit. But I had good cause."

"I'm sorry."

"No, I am. He was supposed to help you. Not rush to judgment and abandon you to handle something of this magnitude on your own."

"Jerk," Mallory mutters.

Director Jacobson nods. Her lips twitch with a repressed smile as she adds, "He had the nerve to demand that I relieve you of your badge and charge you with assault."

"Is that why you're really here?"

"No." She reaches out, setting her hands on my shoulders and giving them a gentle squeeze. Then shocks me when she pulls me into a hug. I'm hyperaware of how bad I smell as she holds me close, whispering, "I needed to see that you were okay with my own eyes, Cassidy."

Releasing me, she adds, "You won't have any trouble from him or anyone at the Miami field office. I've spoken with them, and Agent Richards has been suspended pending an internal investigation. I suspect the outcome won't be decided until it's determined whether or not Mr. Walker will be filing a civil lawsuit for negligence."

"What about me?" I ask. Though I lift my chin, holding my head high, I can barely swallow. "What can I expect?"

"If you're asking about disciplinary action, there won't be any. But if you're talking about recompense,

I've been assured that Agent Richards wants to apologize when you're ready."

The look I give her makes her laugh.

"You are back to your old self, aren't you?"

"Just about."

"That's fantastic news, Agent Knox. I'm glad to hear it. Now what can we do to help?"

"What do you mean?"

Director Jacobson exchanges a look with a grinning Mallory.

"I was told by a rather reliable source that after what happened, you'd be on high alert and that we'd better help take turns guarding your boyfriend."

Mallory gives me an exaggerated wink. "Obviously, we've arrived not a moment too soon 'cause girl, you need to clean up before he wakes up."

I glance down at myself again. I'm beyond filthy. My clothes are stained with dirt, and blood, and something a strange shade of green. And there's no denying that I stink.

But as touched as I am by their offer, as much as this is the very thing that I'd hoped for, the idea of leaving Jake alone right now—even under the director and Mallory's care—for as long as it would take to drive to the sanctuary and back, feels inconceivable. It's too soon. He isn't even conscious yet.

There's a tap on the door, and a nurse sticks her head into the room. "I have the items you asked for, ma'am."

"Thank you."

Director Jacobson gives her a smile and accepts an armful of goods. Once the nurse is gone, she holds them out to me. A part of me crumbles and breaks when I see that she's offering me a pair of clean scrubs, some soap, and shampoo.

"I figured we'd watch him while you use the room's

shower, if that's okay?"

"Thank you," I whisper, my throat growing tight with emotion.

"Oh, and I have your phone." Reaching into her purse with her free hand, she pulls out the device. "The Miami field office downloaded a copy of everything they needed off it, though I'm afraid your car's been seized as evidence."

I give her an appreciative smile as I take the cell and shower supplies from her. Then I retreat into the bathroom and close the door, feeling overwhelmed with gratitude.

The anxiety I'd woken up with is gone. I no longer have to worry about how I'm going to keep Jake safe by myself. Because I'm not alone.

It's a wonderful gift to have received, one that already has me thinking more clearly. There are other responsibilities I need to attend to. Turning on the water to heat up, I dial the number for the local feed store. Drum my fingers against the counter as I wait for the call to be answered.

"Gator Glade Feed and Seed, this is Donna speaking."

"Hi, Donna, this is Cassidy Knox. Butch Donovan's granddaughter."

"I know who you are, honey. What can I help you with?"

"I have a huge favor to ask. Do you think you could help me find someone to hire to feed the animals at the sanctuary?"

There's not even a moment's hesitation before she says, "There's no need to pay someone. I'll go over there myself as soon as I close up tonight. What needs to be done?"

"Thank you, but I can't ask you to do that. It'll be

more than just tonight."

"Is everything all right?"

"It's Jake." My voice is high-pitched and strangled. Though I clear my throat, I still sound strained as I say, "He's been hurt. I'm afraid… I don't want to leave him at the hospital alone. Not yet."

"Is this your cell that you're calling from?"

"Yes."

"I'm texting you my number now. Send me a list of everything that needs to be done, morning, noon, and night. I'll rally the troops. We'll make sure it's all taken care of."

"I appreciate the offer, but I can't expect—"

"Honey, don't you worry about a thing except taking care of Jake. Trust me. I've got it covered. I don't know where you've been these past years, but you're home now, Cassidy. You're not alone in this. You need help, all you have to do is ask."

Tears flood my eyes as I thank her. I'm cloaked in a fog of disbelief as I type up instructions detailing all the animals' diets and routines and hit send. By the time I step under the hot spray of the shower, I feel like an entirely different person.

Because I'm not alone anymore. And neither are they. I'm not sure how I'll ever be able to repay these women who've come to my aid, but whatever they need, whenever they need it, it's theirs.

CHAPTER 45

I feel like I've been in this moment before, wiping my damp palms against my shorts to dry them before depressing the handle. Trying to calm the butterflies in my stomach, which feel like they have fangs. Casting a glance at Director Jacobson and Mallory where they're seated down the hall, I hold my breath and open the door, unsure what I'm going to find on the other side.

But just like the other times I've found myself here, all my concerns vanish the instant I see Jake's face. Well, almost all of them.

I feel timid as I cross the room to his bedside. He looks exhausted. His skin is still too pale, colored only by his bruises and the dark circles beneath his eyes.

"Hey," he says, almost as shyly as I feel.

"Hey."

"Are you okay?" His gaze roams over me, as if searching for the answer. "Things were so hectic before that I don't think I made sure."

"I'm fine. You?" I ask

"Never been better." The grin he gives me turns into a grimace as he adjusts himself on the bed. "It's just my stitches," he assures me, noticing my concerned expression. "I think the doctor pulled them extra tight this time to punish me." Giving me a pointed look, he adds, "If only there was something someone could do to make me feel better.”

I resist the urge to roll my eyes, because for the most part, I’m relieved. If he’s feeling well enough to flirt, then there’s no need to put off what I need to do.

Climbing onto the side of the bed, I straddle him, sitting on his legs above the knees. His gaze widens, his hands sliding up my thighs as he flicks a gaze toward the door.

“Does that thing lock?”

“No.”

“Don’t get me wrong, I like the direction this is going, but what exactly are we doing?”

“We need to talk,” I say.

“Like this?”

“Yes.”

“Is this some kind of FBI interrogation technique? Like, is this what you do when you’re questioning subjects?”

“Nope. Just you.”

Pinching the bridge of his nose, his eyes squeeze shut.

“You’re leaving, aren’t you?” he asks.

“I—what?”

“Listen, I understand. I saw what you can do out there. I get why you wouldn’t want to waste those skills hanging around Gator Glade.”

“I’m not leaving.”

“Then is it me?”

“Yes.”

He swallows hard.

“I am so insanely angry with you, Jake Walker, that I don’t have any idea where to even begin.”

“Cassie, whatever I did—”

“You told me you loved me.”

“I do love you. And you told me you loved me back.

Or, at least, that your heart belonged to me."

"But when *I* said it, it wasn't a deathbed confession."

"Oh."

"Yeah, oh. If you ever pull something like that again—" My voice cracks. I stare at the ceiling, blinking, trying to get my tears to reabsorb. "Why didn't you tell me you'd been stabbed?"

His hands wrap around mine. "I was afraid you would have tried to do something to help."

"I would have!"

"But there wasn't time. Not without putting you in danger."

"Yeah, because it was so safe out there besides that."

"You know what I mean."

"But I don't, Jake. You didn't trust me."

"It had nothing to do with trust."

"It had everything to do with trust. It still does, because now I'm not sure if I can trust you."

"I hate that I made you feel like that."

"Well, you did."

"I'm sorry."

"Do you feel like things are moving too fast between us?"

"What? Where's this coming from?"

Thinking about what Agent Richards said, I add, "I mean, I've been back less than a month and we're basically living together already."

"Do you want us to slow down?"

It's a question I've asked myself multiple times. The rational part of me always answers yes. I know that rushing into a relationship so fast, especially after the losses I've experienced recently, isn't smart.

But this isn't just any relationship. This is Jake. For once, my brain isn't in charge. And according to my heart, there is no too fast.

"No."

"Then help me understand where this is coming from."

I shrug, looking away as I say, "Maybe you didn't tell me you were injured because you wanted to die. Maybe you thought it would be the easiest way to get away from me."

"Cassie, you're being absurd."

"Am I? The agent who was sent to help me find you thought you staged your disappearance as a way out of our relationship."

"And you believed him?"

"If I had, I wouldn't have kept searching for who took you."

"Where is this guy now? I didn't see him out there helping you when everything was going down."

"I sent him away."

"Because you didn't believe him."

"Yes."

"Good." Jake strokes my cheek gently and gives me that lopsided grin of his that makes me feel dizzy. "Because you aren't getting rid of me, Cassidy Knox. I'm all in."

"Yeah?"

He pulls me forward until our lips meet. The kiss he gives me makes my heart skip a beat. Sparks shoot through me. My toes curl inside my shoes.

When it ends, leaving us both breathless, he says, "If I ever do anything to make you think otherwise, I want you to let me know immediately so I can prove to you what's true."

"Like you did just now?" When he nods, I bite my lip, trying not to smile. "I don't believe you really like me at all. Not even a little bit."

I sigh happily as he kisses me again, convincing me I'm wrong, all the strain and worry and fear that's collected inside of me releasing. For the first time in as long as I can remember, I actually believe everything's going to be okay.

Though I'd gladly stay like this all day, I know I need to let him rest. Careful not to jostle the bed, I move to his side and snuggle against him.

"You're incredible, do you know that?" he asks, wrapping his arm around me.

I'm not sure if incredible is a word I'd use to describe myself, but I've come to realize some that are: Strong. Resilient. Determined.

I'm a survivor. No one's ever going to convince me otherwise. And while the time for doubting myself is over, the time for enjoying myself has just begun.

OTHER BOOKS BY SHANNON

CASSIDY KNOX SERIES:

Deadly Sanctuary

CHIEF MAGGIE RILEY SERIES:

The Girl Who Lied
Their Angel's Cry
The Shadow Girl
One Last Sigh
The Day She Died

STANDALONE PSYCHOLOGICAL

THRILLERS:

Best Friends Forever
The Slumber Party
Would You Rather
Her Hiding Place

READER'S NOTE

Dear Reader,

A huge and most sincere THANK YOU for choosing to read FATAL BETRAYAL, the second book in the Cassidy Knox series! With so many books out there to choose from, you have no idea how much it means to me that you chose to spend some of your precious reading time with one of mine, so I have to say it again—THANK YOU!!!!

If you enjoyed FATAL BETRAYAL, I'd be so very grateful if you took the time to leave a rating and/or a review. Even just a few words can have a huge impact on helping other readers to find and choose to read it as well, which would be amazing because I love everything about this series and want to keep bringing it to you for a long time. I can't wait for you to find out what I have in store for Cassidy and Jake!

At the time that I'm writing this, I've just finished the first draft of book 4, book 5 is begging to be let out of my head, and I've become absolutely obsessed with pygmy goats. Seriously. I adore all the animals at the sanctuary, but it's Stephano who has me checking the zoning laws for my yard and researching how hard it is to potty train a goat. (The answer? Hard enough that I'm going to have to write more books first so I can afford more cleaning products.)

If you'd like to keep up with my latest book news and releases, please consider following me on Amazon or BookBub. Even better, sign up for my monthly newsletter via my website (www.shannonhollinger.com) where you can enter to win signed books, find out about contests for additional prizes, make your voice heard by voting on cover designs, titles, etc., become an ARC reader, and so much more! (Your email address will never be shared, and you can unsubscribe at any time.)

Thank you again for your support—it really is hugely appreciated!

Until next time,

Shannon Hollinger

ACKNOWLEDGEMENTS

An incredible amount of effort goes into turning a story into the finished product of a book, and I'm so incredibly grateful that I don't have to do it on my own!

Thank you to Kaycee Racer and her amazing insight into how to make everything she reads stronger and better.

Thank you to Maureen Downey (@booklovermo525) for joining my beta reading team, and to returning victims Heather Flaherty (@thrillology_explorer) and Felecia Mebane (@thebookisdone) for holding my hand through another book. Thank you all so much for being such amazing friends, supporters, and for all you do for the book community!

Thank you to proofreader Melissa Ammons and her "eagle eyes".

Thank you to all the wonderful ARC readers for your reviews!

Thank you to my mom, Stacy, for instilling in me an almost obsessive love of reading from an early age, even if that meant she had to spend years carrying the (momma) lion's share of the books for me.

To my dad, Bob, who never got to see me achieve my dreams, but always believed I would one day. Thank you for never doubting me. I miss you.

To my grandmother, Marvis. Thank you for introducing me to the work of so many great authors. There are so many amazing writers I never would have discovered without you!

Thank you to my husband, Ben, for greenlighting project "Get Shannon a Pygmy Goat" and for not being scared to sleep beside me at night—sometimes quite loudly—despite knowing what I write. You're a brave man, Ben. Brave man.

And mostly, a big, huge, giant THANK YOU to you, reader! I've been writing stories almost since I could write letters, but for years never dared to hope that someone would read them besides my mom. It's because of you that I get to live my dream, and there's no way I can ever thank you enough for that.

My endless gratitude goes to all you readers, reviewers, librarians, booksellers, BookTokers, Bookstagrammers, and everyone else out there who takes the time to share your love of books! You all deserve something special, so go ahead and get that new book you've got your eye on!

Reviews are the most important gift you can give an author, so if you enjoyed your time with this book, please consider leaving a few words, or even just a rating, to help other readers find it as well! Thank you!

ABOUT THE AUTHOR

With degrees in Crime Scene Technology and Physical Anthropology, Florida writer Shannon Hollinger hasn't just seen the dark side of humanity—she's been elbow deep inside of it! She's an avid animal lover, reader, and hiker, and has been known to use her forensic skills to figure out who ate the last cookie in the house.

A multi-genre, Amazon charts top 20 best-selling author, Shannon writes psychological thrillers filled with jaw-dropping twists and shocking endings, the police procedural Chief Maggie Riley mysteries, where the darkness of the Maine wilderness is rivaled only by the deadly secrets it conceals, and the romantic suspense Cassidy Knox mystery thrillers, where the animals will steal your heart and the nights are as hot as the days.

Her novels have been translated into multiple languages, and her short fiction has appeared in Suspense Magazine, Mystery Weekly, and The Saturday Evening Post, among many other magazines and anthologies.

Shannon is a member of the International Thriller Writers and the Short Mystery Fiction Society.

To keep current on book news and to enter monthly giveaways, sign up for Shannon's newsletter through her website, www.shannonhollinger.com.

Find Shannon on social media:

Facebook   @thiswritersays
Instagram   @thiswritersays
BookBub   @shannonhollinger
TikTok   @shannonhollinger
Pinterest   @thiswritersays